BE MY GUEST

BE MY GUEST

Two Novellas

RACHEL INGALLS

Turtle Bay Books
A Division of Random House
New York 1992

LIBRARY OF CONGRESS CATALOGING-IN-PUBLICATION DATA
Ingalls, Rachel.
[Be my guest]
Be my guest : two novellas / Rachel Ingalls.
p.   cm.
Contents: Be my guest — Sis and Bud.
ISBN 0-679-41300-6
I. Ingalls, Rachel. Sis and Bud. 1992.   II. Title.
PS3559.N38B4   1992
813'.54—dc20   91-51044

Manufactured in the United States of America
9 8 7 6 5 4 3 2
First Edition

CONTENTS

SIS AND BUD

Alma and Bruce were adopted. Their adoptive parents, Elton and Bess, had done the right thing and had told them the history of their adoption when they'd turned fourteen: Bruce first, and Alma the next year. Fourteen was the age the agencies had designated for the long, understanding talk that was to be administered with tact and kindness and which had to include at some point the phrase, "You know we love you, because we chose you." Fourteen might not have been the right age for one or the other, or both of them, to learn the facts; nor was it to be supposed that one fourteen-year-old was like another, nor that a girl would have the same attitudes as a boy. But you had to start somewhere.

They each took it differently. Bruce was horrified, infuriated, offended and sickened. Alma was strangely pleased. She began to form the notion that perhaps her mother had been someone very important—maybe even a princess— who hadn't been able to marry her lover for reasons of state, or something like that.

To begin with, they both thought of the true parents as unreal and somehow theatrical or unusual. They didn't feel less warmly towards Bess and Elton: on the contrary, when they'd been told how much their new parents had wanted children, how they'd been disappointed over and over again and how finally they'd been granted the great joy of two such wonderful children, Bruce had been deeply moved. And

Alma had cried and had said she couldn't imagine that her biological parents would ever have been so good to her, even if they were actually the real ones: and she was glad that she'd had the luck to be adopted.

But she began to daydream about the people she now thought of as her real parents: the ones from whose bodies she came in a way that she didn't yet fully understand—the way that was secret, shocking, delicious, immoral, full of pleasures, terrifying and—so everyone kept saying, even though you weren't supposed to do it—natural.

The natural part of parenthood was simply physical. What Bess and Elton had contributed and what their years of patient care had created, was social and cultural. Alma loved them, of course. Yet there was that other element—the mysterious origins that had to do with bodily love and passion. She wondered about the two lost parents: their characters, how long they had known each other. She didn't doubt that they'd been in love. They must have had parents, too; there would be two whole families from whom she had come, not just the two main actors.

As Alma made up stories about this other family of hers, she became increasingly curious about them. Her own imagination supplied the information, as it had invented the questions. She herself was the source and purpose of the drama. In the early stages genuine knowledge would have upset her. She definitely didn't want to find out the truth. There were only two facts that she recognized; the first was that she was now on a different footing with Bess and Elton, so that they seemed more like friends than relatives. And the second was that Bruce was not her real brother, so that therefore there was no reason why they shouldn't get married some day.

She'd always loved him. Now she fell in love with him in another way.

Bruce had had a year to think over the subject without her. When Bess and Elton had had the talk with him, they'd asked him not to tell Alma yet. And he didn't tell. He hadn't told her about Santa Claus, either. Unlike so many older brothers who grow up bullying their sisters and being jealous of them, he'd always tried to shield her. The difference in their size might have had something to do with the development of his protective instincts; she'd been a small, elflike child. Another factor in his response could have been Elton, who entertained a high, idealized opinion of womanhood, and had taken care to guide Bruce towards a desire for the same, rigorous certainty. Elton would have thought of it as one of the treasures of his son's upbringing.

During the year in which he had the time to think about his adoption, Bruce decided: his plan came all at once, not piece by piece. It seemed to him that he'd had a shock and that it had pushed him towards the need to force everything back to the way it had been. As far as he was concerned, his purest and most private feelings had been desecrated. And Elton, whom he'd always thought of as his real father, was not only unrelated but had obviously lied to him about women.

After he'd been told that first time, Bruce never raised the topic again. He thought that it might hurt his adoptive parents' feelings to see him express too much curiosity about the others—as if he hoped that the real ones might have been better or more interesting. He also knew what they'd say. If he asked Elton, "What kind of woman do you think my real mother was?" what could Elton tell him? That she was the kind of woman who went with a man when she wasn't married: who had had an illegitimate child; and that she was the kind of woman who gave her child away to other people.

Up to the age of fourteen Bruce's best subject in school had been history, which had filled his mind with pictures of romantic adventure. All at once he knew what history really was—not just the battles and buildings and heroes, but all the families and how they felt about each other, and how they carried with them distorted versions of each other's lives. He realized that there was private as well as public history. Only the great names lived in such a way that the two merged, but everyone participated somehow in the large, public sweep of historical event. Everyone was influenced, willing or not. He didn't want to be the passive victim of his own life. If you knew where you stood and what you were doing, he thought, you could direct events yourself. He intended to take action, and to run things.

As soon as Alma too had been told, he felt better. He regarded her as an ally in his struggle to come to terms with history. He didn't want to say anything to make her feel crushed, as he had been, but he couldn't understand her gullibility or her willingness to think well of the people who had reneged on their parenthood.

"We don't know," she said. "I guess they could be any kind of people at all."

"She could have been some drunken whore off the waterfront."

"Oh no, the adoption agencies are very careful about who they allow in."

He laughed.

She said, "I think if the mothers don't fulfill certain conditions, the babies have to go into an institution. We've been pretty lucky, haven't we?"

"The hell we have."

"But you'll feel just as close to me, won't you? Even though we aren't really brother and sister now?"

"Who knows? How can you be sure we aren't related? We might be, you know. A man that's had one bastard could have thousands."

"But not a woman."

"No. They only need to have one. That makes them whores."

"How can you say that? Especially nowadays. Nowadays that's all changed. Women can keep their children and bring them up. It used to be impossible. For everybody. Maybe she couldn't marry. Maybe he wasn't free. He could have been already married to somebody else, or he could have died before she knew she was going to have a baby."

"Sure, maybe. Maybe there's icebergs in Africa."

"And maybe she didn't want to get married—have you thought about that? Maybe she was one of those independent career women who just got caught."

"Then she could have had an abortion, couldn't she?"

"That might have been against her religion. It's possible. Maybe the idea of an abortion was worse than going through with the birth."

"No. If you're going to have the baby, you don't give it away."

"Maybe she couldn't afford to keep it. It costs a lot to bring up a child. And if you don't have a job, or some man to support you—"

"Cut it out," he said.

"Well, the way I look at it, I just feel they must have been all right."

"Both of them? Him and her? She might have been some girl your age who was raped by her own father. Or by a whole gang of people."

"Don't say those things. I don't want to think of her like that. And anyway, what about him?"

"Oh," he said, "that doesn't matter."

Alma was already beginning to incorporate her new knowledge into her life. At Christmas she'd been taken to see a ballet about a transformed maiden, brought up by strangers, who had a sister-double who was her moral opposite. And although Alma was the one who was adopted, she had immediately identified the heroine as a character who must resemble her mother: an innocent beauty, preyed upon by evil influences, but in her heart shining and lovely, like a swan. "We might as well think nice things about them," she said, "since we're never going to know."

"We can find out."

"No, we can't. The adoption people never give out information."

"They don't give it out to the real mother. That's so she can't come back and try to squeeze money out of the new family or upset the child by pulling it both ways. But if you're the child, they let you find out about the mother as soon as you're of age. You've got a right to that information. In the state Bess and Elton went to, and according to the adoption place, the age is eighteen, not twenty-one."

She didn't think that could be true. If it were possible to find out, it might even be possible to see the real parents. She said, "Are you sure? Suppose a woman got married after-wards and never told her husband? They couldn't just give you her name and address. You could cause a lot of trouble for her."

"I'm pretty sure they can. It may not be a law. Maybe it depends on the adoption agency. The one we came from al-lows it."

"Did Mom and Dad tell you that?"

"They told me the name and address of the agency be-cause I asked. And then I called up and asked what the policy was. They were a little cagey but they said that if they were satisfied it was a genuine desire to know, they'd tell you. So all we've got to do is wait."

Alma thought about it. She tried to see herself going to an adoption agency to talk with someone there. What were those places like? Maybe they were like hospitals, or maybe it was a clinic with a kind of office attached: the mother could be at one end, giving birth, and, at the other side of the build-ing, the adopting parents would be waiting anxiously, hop-ing that the baby they got would be all right.

If a child were born with something wrong with it, did they hand it back and ask for a refund? Alma imagined Elton and Bess sitting on chairs in a waiting room: Bess would be hold-ing a brown paper bag, to take the baby away in.

She didn't want to think in any greater detail about the procedure. Obviously it was a business—that was the reason why some people did it. The mother would have her hospital bills paid. The agency would get something: a percentage. It was strange to think that she might have cost five hundred dollars, or a thousand, or whatever it was. But she didn't want to ask Bess. She could think about the farcical possibilities without further information and she'd dream about the more mysterious, dramatic and possibly tragic side: the love and character of her mother.

For a long time she never even wondered if her mother had gone on living after giving birth. As soon as the question came to her, she passed it on to Bruce. "You don't think they're dead, do you?" she asked.

"Of course not," he said. "Why?"

"We might have been transferred to the adoption people because our mothers died in childbirth and there was nobody to bring us up."

"I hadn't thought of that, but I don't reckon it's likely. That sounds to me like another case where the orphanage would take over. The kind of place Bess and Elton would go to would be pretty fussy about where they recruited their unmarried mothers from."

"Not off the waterfront, after all? How can you be sure?"

"I suspect they got the name through some religious organization. Don't you think so? First, prevent them from getting hold of birth control and then sell the babies when somebody knocks them up. Wouldn't you say someone like Reverend Hodges would know quite a few convenient little addresses?"

"Not as many as the doctors."

"More. Especially in this part of the country."

"That's another thing: why did they go so far away?"

"Because that's where the adoption place was. And I guess they figured it was a good idea to go to a big city, where they wouldn't run the risk of adopting the child of somebody who could turn out to live right down the road. Both of those women might be there to this day. Or they might have moved away, anywhere: even out of the country."

Alma started to tell herself another story: the search for the mother. She'd think about it in the daytime and occasionally even have a real dream. The mother was always found after long and painful effort and sometimes Alma would arrive too late, just after her mother had died.

ELTON AND Bess were quieter, more formal, more modest and also older than the parents of any of Alma's or Bruce's classmates. They had had to wait a long time until the adoption agency had found the first baby. Many times before that they'd been disappointed. Bruce was their idol until, so soon afterwards, Alma had arrived. They were glad to notice that the news of the adoption didn't seem to have bothered the children. Bruce had become more serious; but that was undoubtedly just because he was growing up. His schoolwork hadn't fallen back—that would have been a bad sign; on the contrary, it had improved. Alma too appeared as outgoing and alert as ever, although sometimes she looked unhappy. Bess had gone out of her way to say that if there was anything Alma wanted to know—anything at all about, say, being a woman—then she could always come and talk to her, or to Dr. Brewster, of course.

"I couldn't talk to a man about anything like that," Alma had said quickly.

"Well then, maybe you could see my doctor. You're too old to keep going to Dr. Brewster now, anyhow."

"Is your doctor a woman?"

"No dear, but he's a gynecologist, so it's all right."

Alma said that she'd wait and see. She wouldn't go back to Brewster, who'd been the family pediatrician, and she didn't see why she had to go to anyone anyway, if there wasn't anything wrong with her. However, she finally agreed to accept the name and address of a woman doctor and to have a complete check-up before the beginning of the next school year.

The doctor's name was Morse; she was married to another doctor. They had three children, two secretaries, a nursemaid, a cook, and a cleaningwoman who came twice a week. One of the daughters was in a lower grade at Alma's school. Mrs. Morse was intelligent, stylish, a first-rate diagnostician of physical symptoms, and someone you couldn't talk to. Alma said she was fine.

"I can see that," the doctor said. "I wish all my patients were so healthy."

Alma smiled, put on her clothes and headed for the door. She didn't ask any of the questions she might have put to an older woman who was also a doctor, for instance: *If a woman gives up her child voluntarily, do you think she's really loved it? If she didn't love it, why did she carry it for nine months? If all that business is as natural as people say, is it natural to take a baby from its mother for any reason whatever? And is it right that a doctor should be helping to say that a childless couple is able to take care of a baby better than its own mother, just because they've got more money than she has? Do you think she could be pushed into giving it away and then change her mind, so she's been thinking about me, so that maybe she wants me to come look for her after all? Do you think she was bad, and that she got pregnant because she was just no good? Am I bad to want to sleep with Bruce: because we were brought up as brother and sister, even though we were never really related? And if we did, is it true what they say—does it hurt a lot, can it make you sick if you do it too much: what's it like?*

Bruce already knew what it was like. He'd wanted to find out without becoming involved, so he'd asked a friend of a friend and he'd made an appointment at a motel with a call-girl. After the first few times, he'd come to an arrangement with her, to see her once every two weeks. It wasn't enough, but he couldn't afford anything more. He hated her, yet she didn't behave hatefully to him; she was ordinary. He couldn't believe how matter-of-fact she was—almost apathetic. It was as if it meant nothing to her, as they said murder meant nothing to psychopaths.

His real mother might have been just like that.

He had dreams about Alma. In his dreams they made love and it was wonderful. He also, once, dreamt about Bess. But he didn't want to have such dreams. His family was his family; it was important that they should stay the way they were. And it was even more vital that his feelings about them should be of a certain nature: filial or brotherly. If they changed, or if he himself did, the idea of the family itself could be altered.

When everybody at school started going steady, he knew that he'd have to have a date, too. He chose the class tramp from the year above him—a coy, lecherous girl with a gobbling laugh, abundant dyed hair and a weasel-like face. He used a contraceptive, as he always had, from the beginning. He said it was because he'd once had gonorrhea and there was a lot of it around. The real reason was that he wanted to be sure he never got a girl pregnant. She told him to take off the rubber because she'd had everything, so she was immune to all that stuff. Then he said that he really wore it because there was insanity in his family, but it skipped a generation: he was okay, but his kids were going to be crazy; it was sad, but true. She believed him until, apparently, she discussed the matter with somebody else. Then she said: Come on, his pa was all right, wasn't he, and nobody ever heard of insanity like that anyway, that skipped. He blew up and said, "Thanks for talking about me with all your friends." And he told her that the reason why he wore a contraceptive was that at least twenty other guys had warned him: If you go down with her, it's like sticking your prick into the town sewer, so watch out. She screamed and hit him in the face. He picked her up and threw her out of the car so that she had to walk home in the dark. They weren't on speaking terms after that.

Alma started going out with boys, but she was shy with them. She didn't want anyone but Bruce. She developed a friendly, joking manner that discouraged romanticism and if that didn't work, she'd just say that she was old-fashioned and intended to save herself for marriage. She started to believe it, although she listened eagerly to what all the other girls she knew had to say about sex. She made up a story that satisfied them, too: she claimed that she'd had a dream about meeting a man four years after highschool and that he would be the one she married. She said that she'd know straight away, and she also knew that none of the boys at school was the right one.

One of her friends, named Penny, said, "I don't see how you can be so sure. I mean, even if you find Mr. Right like that and you get married in a silver cloud and all, why's it going to stop you having some fun now?"

"It wouldn't be fun if he isn't the right one," Alma said.

"Sure it would."

She didn't believe it. She was convinced that you had to be in love. She became moody and short-tempered. She cried a lot. She lost weight and decided that she was going to be a dancer. Bess and Elton agreed to pay for lessons.

BRUCE TOOK UP the violin. He said that he wanted to develop some minor skill that he could use in later life to annoy the neighbors.

"That doesn't sound like a very good reason, dear," Bess said.

"That's because it's a joke," he told her patiently.

He'd saved enough to buy a fiddle that he'd seen in a pawnshop. Bess wanted to know what he'd been doing in a part of town where there were pawnshops. She didn't ask where he'd managed to get hold of the money. He always had money. In the winter he shoveled snow, in the summer he mowed lawns. He'd do deliveries, fix things that were broken, feed pets while their owners were away. He always had some job or other, often several. And he found himself a music teacher by looking through the yellow pages and phoning up one number after another: asking questions, until he'd decided which teachers he wanted to talk to. He settled on a man named Schneider.

He took a lesson twice a week. No one in the family ever met Mr. Schneider but from the sound of Bruce's practicing at home, he seemed to be able to teach a lot of music in a short time. A long while later, Bruce told Alma that Mr. Schneider was a musicology student, only a couple of years older than he was himself—still in his teens. It had amused him to see how everyone, without knowing anything about the man, believed that a music teacher should be ancient, white-haired and, probably, someone who spoke English with a thick accent.

After school Alma would ride all the way across town to do dance exercises in a small room over an art gallery. There was a bar and nightclub next door, a fact that bothered Elton and Bess. But Alma wasn't afraid. She immersed herself in her afternoon practice the way a novice would sink her personality into the formalities of religious training. When men spoke to her on the street or made more determined attempts to pick her up, she took no notice. They tried frequently; she'd turned into a good-looking girl. And the clothes she wore, the way she did her hair, made her seem older than she was.

What she couldn't discuss with her parents she could talk about directly with Bruce. She told him, "You know how I feel. I never said it, but you're the one I want. I used to see you going out with that girl and I hated her so much. You could have gone out with me. You like me: I know that."

"I love you, Alma," he said.

"To marry? Or, we don't have to get married. We could just sleep together."

"No."

"Why not?"

"Because maybe you aren't my sister, but I feel like you are."

"Isn't it ever going to change?"

"No," he said.

"And you'd want me to marry somebody else?"

"Yes, of course. Eventually."

"But I don't want anybody else. I want you."

"You'll find somebody. Listen, if you just want a guy to screw around with, there's the whole world to choose from. But somebody to understand you and give you support in what you think, and be really close to you—that's different."

"That's marriage," Alma said.

"Are you kidding? Marriage is the in-laws and the Thanksgiving dinners and thank-you notes and bringing up the children."

"But you start with love, and working together as a team."

"I can work with men. I don't need that kind of thing. What I need is somebody to be my sister."

"I could be both."

Bruce said, emphatically, no: it wouldn't work to mix things like that. You had to be one or the other. It could ruin everything.

She thought he was right, but she wanted to be the one who wasn't the sister. It didn't occur to her that the whole question of being a sister or a lover, having a real parent and an adoptive parent, feeling love or desire or friendship, was one that could be with her all her life and to which there might not be an answer.

Her teacher, Merle Singer, told Bess that Alma was her best pupil, although she had started so late, and that if she wanted to, she could make her living as a dancer. Three of her pupils, including Alma, had what she considered the perfect physical proportions for a dancer. Some teachers, she knew, held the opinion that the shape of the body determined the nature of the dance, but she had seen too many exceptions—cases where the shape was not conventionally pleasing but the movement was good. Of all her promising students Alma alone stood out. The two who, according to the rulebook, should have equaled her were ungainly and without musicality. When Alma danced, her smallest gestures were charged with meaning and beauty. You couldn't explain something like that simply on the evidence of measurement and ratio. She had the talent. But—just as important—she had the good health, stamina, will-power and concentration to succeed in competition against other girls who might have had better training.

"If you want to go on," Bess said to Alma, "and really try for a career, we'll help you. It means a lot of money at this stage, so think carefully. Merle is sure you can do it, but she talked about the drawbacks too: it's a short working life. You wouldn't have the time or energy for anything else. It's easy to injure yourself—the professional ones sprain and break things all the time. And getting to the top and being famous means a whole series of lucky chances that just might not ever happen. So, you think hard about it."

Bess was proud of Alma. Bruce had the brains; that was a good thing for a boy, but he could be cold, secretive and unforgiving. Neither she nor Elton knew all the time what he was up to. Alma shared herself. And she'd turned out to be beautiful-looking, Bess thought—just like some kind of foreign actress, but underneath it a really nice, down-to-earth girl. Other mothers had daughters who were drinking hard, who were going to bed with just anybody and were being arrested for dangerous driving and all kinds of wild behavior: they didn't care what they did. Elton said you had to blame the parents, but Bess wasn't so sure that that was all there was to it. Some went the wrong road, no matter what you did, and some won through in spite of everything. She and Elton had been lucky. "You know," she said to Alma, "we'll be happy with whatever you choose. It's only a matter of getting the timing right, so you don't spend years working at a thing you're never going to want to use."

"All right," Alma said. "Give me a few days."

She thought over what Bess had said. She liked dancing. She enjoyed the exercise and needed the expression of movement. But the glamor of the stage had never drawn her. Her place was on the other side of the footlights, following the story—that was what she had always loved. And that was something she could have for the rest of her life. If she felt no sense of dedication as a performer, it would certainly be better to stop now.

She told her parents and Merle that she intended to go on doing her exercises in private and maybe taking a class or two every once in a while, but that she was giving up the dance. She was thankful, she said, that she'd had the opportunity to train for long enough to find out that it wasn't the right thing; some girls, she knew, were thwarted by their parents, so that they had the idea forever afterwards that they might have been great artists if somebody hadn't prevented them. She realized that it wasn't the profession for her, even though she was good at it, because there were other things she wanted to do with her life. A girl who wasn't so good, but for whom dancing was the only interest, could give an audience more.

Everyone understood except Merle. Merle said that she

did, but all the time she'd really hoped that Alma would continue; she'd seen her as a star, in the lead role, as the heroine. If she'd known about the family history, she might have fought for her belief and told Alma that the willingness to forsake her talent could well have its beginnings in her conviction that she was not the central character in anything but was, on the contrary, the daughter of a heroine. If you gave dancing lessons to a bunch of clumsy-footed, plain girls who all seemed oddly built and without inborn grace, timing or rhythm, the appearance of a natural champion in their midst was like the arrival of a comet. After one outburst Merle kept quiet, but she couldn't get over the waste of it.

As for Alma, she did what she'd told everyone, occasionally taking a class and continuing to practice on her own. Every two weeks or so she'd drop in on Merle to have a cup of tea or coffee and to chat. It was a while before she realized that it was her lost career that weighed on Merle's mind, and not perhaps the loss of revenue that might mean so much: Merle had two teenage boys and a divorced husband who was always ducking out of the alimony. By the time Alma understood that another person—of an age to be her mother—had had great expectations of her, she was too far away from her decision to feel guilty about causing the disappointment.

Twice a year, around Christmas and just before summer, she went with Merle on a weekend expedition to the big city, where they saw the Saturday matinée and evening performances of a ballet. For the whole day she'd live in a world of princesses and sorcerers, enchanted maidens, magical animals and demons.

She began to think of Bruce's predicament in terms of the

stories she'd seen on stage. He too was living under a spell and was unalterably persuaded of the necessity of breaking it. There was a willingness to disbelieve, Alma thought, that could be just as potent a force as the need for faith. Bruce had that. He thought that when he found the real parents, when they were confronted with the outcome of their actions—with the sight of him—they'd disappear. It would be as if they had never been. He would then be like a god: someone who had been brought into the world without the aid of parents. He was willing to waste himself and the whole of his life on his obsession, just as she would waste herself on him.

BRUCE KEPT a diary. He'd started it at the age of ten, beginning with descriptions of what had happened during the day, of the food he'd eaten, the clothes people were wearing and the state of the weather. Seasonal phenomena were also noted: ice storms, trees in flower, leaves turning color. That stage didn't last long. He skipped days; then he began to use the diary for ideas that had occurred to him, stories he'd been told, interesting facts he'd read, and, in the end almost exclusively, for his dreams.

When he was fourteen, he wrote in the diary:

If people are really in trouble, even atheists, they call on God. They all know what that means. They say to themselves, "Oh God, get me out of this. Oh God, help me—save me." The idea of God comes from deep inside them. It may be caused by their fear, or it may be a wished-for aspect of themselves that would be capable of controlling the hopeless situation as their parents once ordered the world for them. But everyone recognizes what's meant by the idea.

It must have something to do with the catastrophic side of life, which there's no way of avoiding. You have to give it a name.

ONCE THE NUMBER of her dance classes had been cut down, Alma spent more time with Bess. She asked to learn how to cook, to sew and to knit sweaters. Unlike most schools in larger towns, hers had never had a domestic science course. It was taken for granted that girls would be taught all those accomplishments at home and that boys wouldn't need to know them. The only sewing Alma had ever done was repairwork on her ballet shoes and mending her tights. She'd always bought anything that Bess couldn't supply. Bess, who took pride in her own domestic skills, hadn't wanted to interrupt Alma's life with home chores. She'd thought that Alma could pick up those things when she got married.

For a while the dinner table saw new dishes half-crumbled or partly burned, cakes that looked like sponges and pies that had suffered a cave-in. But Alma was quick to learn. She liked to cook. Soon she was pushing the family to experiment with more exotic foods and flavors. She also enjoyed the evenings when she and Bess sat sewing or knitting and Elton read the papers. Elton could read a paper straight through a conversation, although every once in a while he'd put it down to listen or join in.

Alma used to ask questions about Bess's early life, about the grandparents and other relatives she'd never met because they'd died while she was still too young to remember anything. Bess had a fund of ghost stories too, which Alma loved to hear her tell again and again. Elton knew only two frightening stories, both supposed to be true: one about a

man who was struck by lightning, and the other a
howling dog that gave the clue to who had murde
owner. Elton was impressed by true stories, or rath
stories he read in the papers. Sometimes he'd laugh
announce in the middle of talk, "It says here . . ." and u
he'd end up by asking, "Would you believe it?" or "How
that!"

BRUCE WAS the class heart-throb at school. He went out
everybody. The phone never stopped ringing for him. "I
day," Bess said, "we didn't chase boys. They don't lik

"They love it," Alma told her. "They love having a fan
and playing the field. So do girls."

"Well, you don't."

"Nope. And just about everyone in my grade thinks the
something wrong with me."

"Nonsense. You're a nice, old-fashioned girl."

"They call it frigid."

"I never heard of such a thing. It wouldn't hurt some
them to get a little frigid for a change. You'll see—you'll
glad when the right man comes along and you didn't thro
yourself away."

Bess didn't bother to give Bruce advice; neither did Elto
They both suspected the sort of thing he might be doing, an
knew that he could handle whatever trouble he got into. He
was like a grown man, although he was so young. He was
ambitious too, in school and out. He'd learned a lot from
working with Elton in the hardware store; then he helped
out at the garage they went to. He fixed people's cars, radios,
TVs, clotheswashers—anything. He'd bought an old car from
a junkyard and made it practically like new. He was success-

ful in everything. Even the teachers admired him. But his classmates weren't close to him. If he sometimes led them to believe that they were, his friendliness was merely diplomatic. Nor did his girlfriends touch him at all deeply. He didn't give himself away emotionally. He didn't reveal his true mind. He stood aside.

Elton and Bess often felt shy about talking to him. They used to get Alma to ask him questions they wanted answered or to tell him things "for his own good." He'd take anything from Alma.

Alma was now his lieutenant and his right hand, almost his other self. As soon as he'd started to go out with so many girls, she knew that he wasn't going to be interested in any particular one for long. When his dates called up, she'd answer the phone and pretend to be sympathetic. Even the ones who knew that she and Bruce were adopted assumed her to have nothing but a sisterly interest in him. As for him, he'd said to her that all his dating was unimportant. It was like having an itch and scratching it: it made no impression on his feelings or his thought, or anything that made him a person.

She told him that she was glad to hear that, because she didn't see why she shouldn't start going out seriously herself. "It's different for a girl," he said quickly. "I wouldn't want you to get hurt."

"You wouldn't want me to have fun, even though you don't want me yourself."

"That isn't true," he said.

"You're never going to want me, are you? It's worse than being in love with a man who doesn't like women. In your case, there's no reason."

"I don't think I'm capable of loving too much anyway. It isn't in my temperament. Honestly. I don't understand what people mean by it. And what I think maybe they've got in mind—that strikes me as being totally uninteresting and false."

"How do you mean?"

"Oh, the usual gooey hearts and flowers stuff."

"When you were little, you loved all that kind of thing. You were a very tender-hearted little boy."

"Was I? Well, things have changed. What I want, Alma, is for you to be on my side."

"Aren't I always?"

"You know what we said: about finding our parents."

"Oh."

"Tracking them down."

"I still think—"

"You promised," he reminded her.

She said yes, she'd promised. And she repeated the promise: she'd help him. As soon as they were old enough, he'd said, they'd go to the adoption clinic and find out about their parents. He'd get there first, naturally, and she'd go the next year. They'd swear to help each other find the missing parents—that is, the mothers. The fathers, in Bruce's opinion, didn't seem to carry so much blame, even supposing that the women knew who the fathers were.

They'd had a long conversation on the subject about eighteen months before, after she'd refused to see or speak to Bobby Paling. Bruce was the one to answer the phone then. Once Alma had substituted her two surrogate mothers, Bess and Merle, for the friendship of girls her own age, she'd become isolated from part of school life. Her attitude towards boys had further estranged her from schoolfriends, so for a while—just to have someone as an excuse—she'd gone out with two of the class duds. They'd turned out to be even more desperate for sex than the attractive ones. Her standard defense to suggestive maneuverings had always been the reply, "Why should I?" Bobby Paling's answer to that was "Because I want to." He was nervous, skinny and tripped over his own feet, but his approach to the opposite sex was fearless. Outside school his main interests were building model ships and trying to find someone else who had Victorian lead soldiers from the regiments he was missing. After Alma had said that she never wanted to see him again, the girl at the desk to the left of hers told her that, according to the other boys, he also had a huge collection of pornographic magazines.

Bruce thought the episode was funny. He'd lean back in the front-hall chair and murmur into the phone that his sister had happened to mention that very morning how Bobby reminded her of the rear end of a baboon.

"I thought you'd given that up," she said.

"Why?"

"I don't know. I thought you'd sort of cooled down. Are you really going to try to find out?"

"You bet I am. Aren't you?"

"I don't think so. Why do you want to?"

"To hunt them down and pay them back."

"What for?"

"For ruining my life."

"But they haven't done anything to your life."

"That's right," he said. "That's just the kind of thing I mean."

"I don't understand it. If someone had done you a wrong, or betrayed you—"

"What greater wrong could there be? What betrayal could be worse?"

"It might have been worse for them than for you. Especially now. You've got a full life without them. But they'll always be wondering about you. At least—maybe not your father. But she would: I'm thinking about your mother."

"So am I."

"And I don't think you ought to allow yourself to become so wild about other people and their quarrels. If I were in one of those law cases people are always pulling on each other, I'd just pay up and get out, no matter how much in the right I was. Otherwise they dominate your thoughts and emotions for years."

"So, if somebody attacked you in the street, you'd just drop it, would you?"

"I didn't mean that kind of thing. I meant grievances, arguments."

"Same principle."

"Why do you want to throw away your life on something that's past? It isn't even your past. It's theirs."

"It's mine. And it's mine because of them."

"It's—"

"It's no use talking about it."

"—like picking a scab."

"That's right. I can't help it."

She couldn't talk to him about it. She didn't even under stand what he meant, though she was glad that he was willing to confide in her. She'd help him, she said, if that was what he wanted. But for herself—she didn't really think she'd want to know the truth. If she did ever meet her real parents, it would be so much too late for all of them; that was probably why the adoption societies insisted that you had to be legally of age before you could get hold of any information: after a certain point, you were just no longer a child. You'd be more willing to understand. You'd be able to think about things objectively. At least, that would be the general idea. Alma didn't believe that Bruce was going to change his mind. The plan of somehow getting back at his parents had taken root. It wasn't going to vanish. It would grow. You could hear a special tone and emphasis in his voice when he talked about it. He thought of it as a quest.

Once he was talking about it to her and he started to sound so vicious that she said, "It makes me feel bad to hear you talk like that. It's tearing you up. Maybe you should go see somebody about it."

"Who?"

"I don't know. A doctor, maybe."

"Why should I go to a doctor? What's wrong was wrong with them, not me. Did it help you to go to that doctor?"

"I didn't get so wound up about everything."

"Sure, you did. You only show it in a different way. I'm just fine. Don't come up with any more dumb suggestions like that."

"I don't like to see you getting upset, that's all. I can listen, but I don't know how to help."

"You help by listening. That's the whole deal. Don't worry about me."

"Sometimes I think you want to kill them."

"Listen," he said. "I'm supposed to be writing a history

essay at the moment. You know what they tell you—great history is great interpretation. There's no other way to examine it. You can plot it all so intricately, and then there are these sudden upheavals that there's no reason for. You can't even see them coming. You can only start tracing it back and then say to yourself: Well, that was a sign. But that would be the kind of clue you'd get from talking to someone who's insane. It wouldn't help to predict what he's going to do next. It doesn't point out where any future burst of power is going to come from. That's the secret. I can really understand why politicians go crazy for power. It's the urge to be able to change history, to guide it or redirect it. Imagine if you could do that. You'd change the world. If you could get people to follow your ideas, you could reshape the world in your own image. Couldn't you?"

Alma said, "What would the world be to me, if it was only myself? The world is other people, Bud. It's the outside. It isn't home."

"Sometimes I just don't feel that I belong here."

"Of course you do. We all love you."

"I mean, I don't feel that I belong anywhere. That I belong anywhere on this earth."

"If you're alive, you belong here. Everybody does."

HE WAS the hero of the school playing fields and the star of every class play. He was a good actor, both for serious and comic parts. He also had a fine singing voice. In his junior year he was running the school paper. In the summer he worked hard at different jobs, mainly on construction sites, where he earned a lot of money. Parents who might not have liked his fast reputation with girls approved of his diligence and initiative. When he suggested to Alma that she should come on a tour of hospitals with him to demonstrate dance steps to the patients while he played the violin, the community was astounded by his sense of civic responsibility. No one in town had ever thought of such a scheme. He said that he got the idea from reading about nineteenth-century mental asylums that held regular concerts for their inmates; the music, he'd read, soothed and delighted the audience. Just recently he'd also heard somewhere that hospitals in Scandinavia maintained the practice. The school principal and the board became enthusiastic about his idea. They took the entire school band on a charity tour of hospitals. Meanwhile, once a week, on his own, he played the fiddle while Alma danced and Merle explained the steps to their audiences. In Bruce's last year a boy named Richard was added to their group; he wasn't an especially good dance partner but he was strong enough not to drop Alma and he didn't mind the idea of playing to a roomful of confused, crippled, dying or possibly insane onlookers.

Alma loved the hospital sessions because of Bruce. She knew how the idea had come to him and why: because he recognized the irrationality of his obsession and perhaps feared that there was something in his own inheritance akin to the conditions suffered by many of his listeners. He treated the patients as if they were normal. He was absolutely relaxed with them. She wondered why he'd never thought of becoming a doctor. Bruce laughed at the idea. He didn't want to help anyone, he said: he wanted to have their attention, that was all.

He won a scholarship to the college he'd set his sights on.

He told Alma, and no one else, that he'd gambled with a large part of his savings and had won, making so much money that he could travel all over the world, if he had to. That meant that if his real mother turned out to live in China or India or Australia, he'd still be able to get at her.

Last night I had a dream that I was sitting at my desk, reading one of my history books: one that I'd never seen before. It was full of colored illustrations, like the books we used to have when we were children. I was turning the pages and looking at scenes from ancient Egypt, from classical Greece and Imperial Rome. And as I looked at them, each page became like a kind of box, inside which a scene of history was being acted out. They were like little theaters that you could look into and, as you watched the plays going on inside, you could listen to them too. While I was turning the pages, the scenes became more and more fascinating and beautiful and real, until suddenly I was in one of them myself.

I was in a medieval castle, where there was eating and drinking and some music playing from the gallery. People were helping me to put on a chain-mail shirt and metal shinguards. Then I was in a courtyard with the other knights. We got on our horses and rode off to battle. The ride was terrific— fast and breathless, and we went thundering through a forest of gold trees. I thought that I'd entered a fairytale, but the man next to me pointed ahead at a large, dark mountain in the distance. As we neared it, I could see that it was coming at us with a speed greater than ours. The man said, "It's The Tide of History." As soon as we got close to it, it reared up and went over us like a wave. It was thick and smothering—a horrible kind of mud. But you could cut it with your sword. So we kept

hacking all around us, kicking wedges of the stuff away from
us. But it was also pulling us down into itself. It was trying to
grab hold of me. I got scared. And then I saw that it wasn't
mud. It was blood. It was the blood of all the people who had
ever been killed and of all the ones who weren't born yet. It
was uncontrollable. I wanted to get away from it, but I
couldn't. And I woke up, staring into the darkness.

The adoption agency was housed in a one-story building of
municipal brick. It looked as if it could have been a bank, a
fire station or even a chapel. He thought it was fitting that
everything about the place should appear anonymous.

He'd written ahead and he'd dressed for the part: neat, re-
spectable, mature. He was good at interviews: they gave him
a chance to display his acting talents. And he wasn't going to
make any mistakes. He'd told himself that if the bastards saw
he had a hair out of place, they'd probably refuse him the
information, or just lie and say that they didn't have it.

The woman who interviewed him was in her early fifties
and not good-looking, although she too had taken care with
her appearance, mainly with her hair, which looked almost
sculpted. She had his file on the desk in front of her. It
crossed his mind that if she really said no, he could knock
her out, grab the file and just run. Why not? This was going
to be his only chance to get his hands on the records. No
court would convict him because a jury would understand a
man's need to know the truth about his past. And an adoption
agency would be very careful about getting into a tangle with
the law, maybe hitting the headlines.

The woman's name was Mrs. Whitlow. A sign on her desk said so, as did a plastic card pinned to the cardigan she'd draped over her frilly blouse. "Well, Bruce," she said, "why do you want to find out about your natural parents?"

"Just because of that," he told her. "Because no matter what, they are my parents by nature. I guess you could say I feel that things have got to be settled. My parents have been great. If I'd never known, it wouldn't have made any difference to me. But when they did tell me, I knew then that I'd always want to know more about the others."

"Yes," she said, "I see."

He could tell that he'd made a good impression. She put her hand on the file and turned the cover. His breathing speeded up a little.

"There isn't too much we can tell you," she said, and stopped.

He gritted his teeth and waited. She seemed to be reading. He concentrated on keeping his voice right, and asked, "Were they married?"

"No." She looked up. "I'm afraid we have no information at all about the father."

"Well," he said gently, "anything you can tell me."

"The mother's name was Joanna Elizabeth Henderson. She was sixteen."

Despite all the possibilities he'd gone over in his mind so many times, he'd expected to hear that she'd been in her thirties, or possibly late twenties: a woman—someone who could take care of herself and who knew what she was doing. Not a young girl.

Mrs. Whitlow continued, "Fifteen, when her parents first came to us, in 1962. It seems that there was an unsuitable alliance, with a married man. Yes. We talked to the girl. She was hostile but not hysterical. She agreed that adoption was the best course. She knew that without the help of her parents, she'd be in the hands of the courts. Underage, no means of support . . ."

He felt sick for a moment as he wondered if the interview could have taken place in that very room, where the low ceiling added to the sense of claustrophobia. It was certainly possible that other rooms down the corridor held pregnant girls and worried parents, who didn't want to become grandparents. He would have liked to know if anyone in the family had expressed regret about giving the baby away. It wasn't a question for asking eighteen years later.

Mrs. Whitlow said, "That's all I can tell you."

"If you don't mind, I'd like to know quite a few practical details. Medical history, that kind of thing. Have I inherited anything that I should know about?"

"Everything was perfectly normal, so far as we could tell."

"On my father's side, too?"

"That we don't know, but we did receive an assurance from the family doctor that there was nothing out of the ordinary in his history."

"His family doctor? Or hers?"

"It's the same name on both reports."

"They had the same doctor?"

"So it appears."

"Then they must have had a record of the name."

"Yes." She flipped to a section in the file, looked through a few sheets of paper and turned back the cover again. "There's nothing here. It does seem strange, but not completely unheard of. There may have been reasons. I just don't know. We have the name of the doctor, but not of the patient. And no medical record, only a statement that the examination showed nothing unusual."

"Right. Well, in that case, if that's all, I wonder if you could let me have the address she was living at when she came to see you."

"You're going to try to make contact?"

He smiled one of his dozen best smiles, saying, "Oh, I don't think so. I told you: my parents are enough. But I really do have the feeling that I'd like to find out about the others. I guess it's because my field is history."

"Oh," she said. And after a moment she simply took the file and turned it around so that he could see, and copy out, everything.

He wrote down all the names and addresses: town, parents, daughter, doctor, and so on. His handwriting seemed to him jerky and strange-looking. Mrs. Whitlow sorted through some papers of her own while he was busy. When he'd finished, he stood up. He thanked her and said that she'd been a big help. His face and voice were composed as he left the room, went down the hallways and came out of the building.

He walked straight to his car, as if he had somewhere to go. All his movements retained a look of purposeful coordination.

He drove the car around a couple of corners, just to put some distance between himself and the adoption agency. He parked under a tree.

He sat behind the wheel and sweated. He started to shake. He didn't understand what was happening to him. The whole of his face was suddenly wet. He put his hands up to cover his eyes. He couldn't stop.

It lasted for about three minutes. There was a point where he was afraid that he wasn't going to be able to get himself out of it. He tried to think. He tried to tell himself to relax. It couldn't be. It ought not to be possible: that he, who was always perfectly in control of himself, should fall apart.

When it was over, he felt exhausted. He wished that Alma were with him, right at that moment, sitting on the seat next to him. They could begin the search now. He had all the information he'd needed.

He thought: Maybe Joanna Elizabeth hadn't known the man was married. She could have been taken for a ride. Maybe. There hadn't been anything about religion in the files. That had surprised him. If a fifteen-year-old, middle-class girl went ahead and had a child, you'd think that there would be some religion in the background, especially since the girl hadn't intended to keep the baby. On the other hand, he'd known quite a lot of fifteen-year-old girls himself and not all of them were angels. Some of them had been doing it since they were twelve. Some charged money for it. It was certainly a possibility that she'd gone after this married man and tried to blackmail him, or had done it to spite her parents, or something like that. The man had had the same doctor: that would make it a lot more likely that all these people were known to each other, and that she'd be aware of the fact that he was married. And he wouldn't necessarily have to be her parents' age, either. He could have been under thirty. Still—it shouldn't have happened: for her to have a child and then ditch it.

He started to tap his hand against the steering wheel. "No," he muttered. His hand beat down more violently on the wheel, again and again. He wasn't aware of it, nor of his voice repeating the word "no," until he hit the horn by mistake.

Stop, he told himself. *This is idiotic. Facts first; then start to think about it. Never theorize ahead of the data: that's the rule for historians. It should be the rule for everyone.*

He started the car. The sky was still clear, the trees in leaf, the houses evenly spaced along the road. Nothing was out of place. Given a little luck, anyone ought to be able to find his way in such a well-regulated world.

HE TOOK Alma out for a meal at her favorite Italian restaurant. They sat in a booth away from the other diners. He purposely didn't order any cocktails or wine. He wanted to keep calm and get everything in the right order.

"It was simple," he told her. He described Mrs. Whitlow. He repeated what he'd discovered. "Now," he said, "we just find out if anybody's living at that address—if they died, if they moved, if they changed their names, and so on. Twenty years ago it wouldn't be so easy. Now everybody's on a computer somewhere."

"They didn't say anything about your father? No name or anything?"

"No. I don't know why I expected it. Bastards don't usually know the name of their father."

"Don't keep calling it that."

"Why not? It's the truth. Anyway, I'm having second thoughts about the married-man story. Maybe she didn't know who it was. Maybe she was just one of nature's whores."

"Bruce, whatever she was, she was your mother."

"Uh-huh."

"She could also have been a girl whose parents disapproved so much, they sort of forgot to tell her about birth control. You know what I mean? There are a lot of them left, even now. And in those days, you couldn't get anything legally, unless you were a man. A doctor would report you to your parents, otherwise he'd get into trouble. It was against the law."

"Sounds a little far-fetched to me."

"I don't like it that you've got this feeling of hatred against her."

"Joanna."

"You had it before you even went to the agency. It isn't good to think like that, Bruce."

"You're just nicer than I am. What I feel is that there are some people who always get away with it—always. And they shouldn't be allowed to."

"Do you really think a woman who's had an illegitimate child has gotten away with anything?"

"She could have stayed with us. With me."

"Oh, Bud. Way back then? Even nowadays—at the age of fifteen, with her parents about to throw her out of the house?"

"Well, if she couldn't, then she should have had an abortion."

"I guess in those days they weren't so easy to get. And it would have cost a lot of money. And maybe it would have been too dangerous."

"I think she was just a bitch, that's all."

Alma reached across the table and grabbed his hand. "Stop," she hissed at him. "Stop it, right now."

He laughed. "Right. It isn't that important."

"And it was over a long time ago."

"I'm still going to find out, though. Aren't you?"

"Maybe. I don't know."

"Well, do what I did: just go there and see what they can tell you. You don't have to do anything about it. You could even think about it for ten years before you follow it up."

"Is that what you're going to do?"

"I'm starting now. I wouldn't want to leave it and then find out they'd died just the week before I rang the front doorbell."

"If we'd never been adopted," Alma said, "I'd never have met you."

"Probably not."

"We could do other things besides look for our parents. We could travel around the world together. We could get married."

"I told you: I'm not getting married."

"I bet you will."

"And I can't start making plans about anything else till I get this out of the way."

"So, you wouldn't mind if I got married to somebody else?"

"Who?"

"How do I know? I could meet somebody at any minute."

"Oh. Well, when you're ready to settle down, I guess that'll be up to you. But you promised to help me if I need you to go in and get information for me."

"Yes," she said. "Sure."

● ● ●

IN THE BALLETS, Alma thought, it was always the woman at the center of the drama. She was lifted high, carried into the light, put where you could see her displaying herself like a preening bird. But life was the reverse. In love, in marriage, she was supposed to be in the background, coming second. She was waiting by the stove or standing at the front door, tapping her foot and thinking: *Where are you? If you were going to be late, you could have called.* She was the one who loved and he was the one who didn't care. Why wasn't Bruce ever going to love her?

What brought her almost to despair was the thought that if she didn't care so much, he might begin to consider her interesting or romantic: if she were unaffected by him, if she felt nothing. But she'd never be able to pretend that. Her feeling for him was always boiling up in her to the point where it blocked out other people. It spoiled everything. All the wonderful things she had—the good luck, the loving parents, the nice life—weren't enough. The only thing she'd ever wanted was never going to be hers.

And her mother? Her mother had taken one step further. In her case it hadn't been just that the one wanted prize was withheld. No. The one unwanted calamity had come upon her and she'd had to accept it. Even though the evidence had been disposed of.

But perhaps her mother hadn't thought of it like that. Who could tell?

HE DIDN'T NEED her at all in the beginning. He only wanted her to listen to him as he reported back the things he'd found out: The Hendersons, his grandparents, were still in the same house. He could go and take a look at them any time, if he wanted to. The daughter, Joanna, had run off to Maryland when she was eighteen and married a man called Raymond Baxter, who was ten years older than she was.

"Well, maybe they're happily married somewhere," Alma said.

"Maybe she's been divorced and remarried six times by now."

"And they could have children of their own."

"What?"

How could his mother have had other children, when she'd thrown away the first one? She'd have no right to do such a thing. He didn't think she'd have the right to be happily married, either. "Well, we'll see," he said.

He went away to college. He studied hard. He got top grades. Alma too applied herself to her schoolwork. She didn't see the sense of working at anything, but she knew that if she didn't push herself, she'd give up completely. Every day, from the beginning to the end, she missed Bruce. Time passed without enjoyment for her, so that when she looked back at the year, long stretches of it seemed never to have been.

ALMA MEMORIZED her lines for the school play, *The Importance of Being Earnest*. She had the part of Gwendolen, the sophisticate. The part of Cecily, the sweet, unspoiled girl, had been given to the class flirt, who played it surprisingly well.

After rehearsals she'd rush back home to see how Bess was. Bess had started to have fainting spells; her doctor, Dr. Mason, said that they were caused by blood pressure. He'd given her some pills, but she still got tired out and would feel faint. At last Dr. Mason referred her to another man, a doctor named Boyd. Elton told Alma that Dr. Boyd was a specialist in heart diseases, and that in fact there had been a lot of heart trouble in Bess's family; she'd never mentioned it: she didn't see why she should upset the children. "But modern medicine," Elton said: "They can work wonders. They've even got these little pacemaker gadgets."

"Oh, my God," Alma said, "is it that bad?"

"No, honey. Don't fly off the handle. I'm just telling you: if. You know what heart conditions are like. People can last up into their nineties so long as they take good care of themselves."

Or they can go at any minute, Alma thought. She telephoned Bruce. "I don't want to worry you," she told him. "I just wanted to hear your voice, that's all. Dad says I'm getting too worked up about it. Anyway, she's not feeling so good. And that's why."

Bruce said that he'd be back in two weeks for a visit. He called up the next day to say hello. When Alma came home from school she found Bess pleased and cheerful.

"He'll be here next week," Bess said.

"That means next month."

"Well, at least he's keeping in touch."

"It's the thought that counts," Alma said.

"That's right."

"But actions speak louder than words."

"Alma, you're teasing."

"I think he could come home a little more often than he does. He can afford it."

"It makes a big difference in the house. Even when he was so busy with something, and he'd just march right upstairs without saying a word: at least he was here. He said if he couldn't make it, he'd be home for your birthday, definitely."

BESS WAS well enough to attend the school play. She applauded vigorously. "Wasn't it just the best thing?" she kept telling everyone: "Wasn't it fun? You couldn't see anything better on a professional stage." Elton's enthusiasm almost surpassed hers. He'd loved everything: the story, the laughs, the other players and the costumes. He kept saying how pretty Alma had looked in her dress. He thought that they ought to let her keep it.

Bruce was busy and didn't come. He sent a telegram instead. Alma felt that he'd let her down. He never missed something he really wanted to see.

All the time everyone had been praising and petting her, she'd been looking at the door or listening for the telephone; hoping for him.

After that, she didn't believe that he'd turn up for her birthday.

THE NIGHT before her birthday, she had a dream. In the dream she went to visit Bruce in the hospital. She entered a room where he was sitting up in bed, reading. A long tube like a garden hose came out of his chest and plugged in to a machine that stood by the bed. "Is it your heart?" she asked him. And he said, "That's right. The machine replaces what the heart used to do. I'm going to have to be on it for the rest of my life." She said, "Aren't I going to see you any more?" "Of course," he told her. "You can come visit me any time you like."

• • •

BRUCE CAME home, bringing presents for everyone. They had a party for Alma and the day afterward he drove her up to the city for a weekend of shows and celebration.

They went to a play, a musical, two movies; to the zoo and the park. And to the adoption agency. She didn't realize where they were headed until he parked down the street and told her which building it was. He'd made the appointment for her, so everything was fixed. "If you don't take the trouble to find out now," he said, "you never will—I know you. You'll just sit around all your life, wondering about what your mother was like and what she's doing now." He reached across her and opened the door. He pushed her until she got out. Then he leaned forward and slammed the door behind her. She moved away, not really knowing where she was going. All she could think of was that he shouldn't have sprung it on her like that. He should have given her warning. Now that they were there, she supposed that she'd better go in.

All the way down the sidewalk and up the path to the building, she was nervous. But as soon as she stepped through the doorway, she thought: *He's right. I don't have to do anything with the information but at least I'll have it, just to know. And they can't refuse it to me, because it's my right.*

She saw a different woman from the one Bruce had described. This one was named Roberts; she was plump-faced and sandy-haired and had a businesslike manner. She asked why Alma wanted to find her parents. Alma said she wasn't certain that she did.

"When I was younger," she explained, "I was sure I never even wanted to know about them. But I've changed. Now I'm curious. I'd also like to know medical things; every doctor I go to comes up with these questions like: Did my mother have heavy periods? and that kind of thing. The family history. And I do sometimes have the feeling that I'd like to know what my mother looked like. If you've got a photograph? And to have her name and maybe address—then, if I ever did want to meet her, I could write to her first. Or maybe I'd never do anything. But I'd have the choice."

There was no photograph, and again, as in Bruce's case, no information about the father, except that he'd been young. The pregnancy had been the outcome of a highschool romance. Both sets of parents had apparently discussed the matter and everyone had agreed that the two young people weren't old enough to take on the responsibilities of marriage and children; they were still underage and supported by their families.

"How sad," Alma said. "For all of them."

"It's a story we hear a lot," Mrs. Roberts said, "even now. Sometimes it's like taking a dare, to show their parents they're grown up. And then they get in too deep and find out it's really too much for them to handle." She passed a piece of paper across the desk.

Alma took the paper and started to read. Her mother's name was Rose Ellen Parker. The last address the adoption society had was that of her family's house in Connecticut. The medical facts appeared to be straightforward and the birth had been without complications. Everything had been completely usual.

"Except," Mrs. Roberts said, looking down at her papers, "that afterwards . . . but that's normal, too. There's a certain amount of time you have to allow. For adjustment."

"Whose adjustment?" Alma said.

"Well, everybody's, actually. The new parents, too."

"But whose did you mean just now?"

"There's a note here about subsequent interviews with the girl, Rose. She was unhappy with the situation."

"She wanted me back?"

"I wouldn't read too much into it. A reaction one month later is one thing. Ten years later might be different. She might feel relieved that she'd done the right thing. You see, it isn't easy for anyone involved. We just try to do the best with what we're handed. Our first concern has to be the welfare of the child."

"Yes," Alma said. She was glad, all over again, that she'd been brought up in a complete family, with a mother and father and brother, instead of being raised as the illegitimate burden of a single teenager and her disappointed parents.

She folded the paper, put it in her purse and shook hands with Mrs. Roberts.

For the short time it took her to walk down the corridor, she continued to feel that something had been settled. But as soon as she stepped out into the sunlight, it seemed to her that nothing had changed.

She walked to the car and got in. "Well," she said to Bruce, "that's that."

"I'm going to buy you a drink," he told her. "I sure as hell needed one afterwards."

They had the drink, and then a second one, and he took her on to another place, where they ate lunch. Alma told him what she'd found out. He asked if they'd given her the name of her father, too.

"The name, but nothing else. James Ridler, Rickman—something like that. I've got it here."

"If they were in the same school, it should be easy to trace them both."

"Would they tell me if she'd kept on trying to get me back? I mean, for years?"

"I doubt it."

"They should have some organization for adopted people to talk about things with each other. I can't imagine what it would be like on your own."

"I'm sure they do. Why not? They've got everything else. Just give me the names and addresses and I'll do the rest."

"What?"

"I'll find out where she is."

"Have you found yours?"

"Yes. A couple of weeks ago."

"And?"

"I wasted a lot of time at the start, beginning at the beginning. Her parents are still alive somewhere up in New England. So's the doctor in the case, who was married to her mother's sister. Her father was a different kind of doctor; a bacteriologist. I think it's safe to assume that the parents hired their in-law to hush up the name or the facts, or both. Unless I'm the outcome of one of those dismal family passions you hear about. But I don't think so."

"You could go see them and find out."

"I could. But there's no point. I can find out from her. I know where she is. That was the hard part. Joanna Elizabeth. She and her husband started a second-hand car firm, then a garage and a taxi service, then a car showroom.

They've branched out into horseracing, stud farms, who knows what else. He's a crook."

"You can't know that. Second-hand cars aren't always a cheat. And horses—"

"He was in jail."

"Are you sure?"

"It's on the records."

"What was it for?"

"Rape. Mummy knows some real nice folks."

"Maybe it wasn't really—"

"Oh, maybe. Anyway, like I said, she got married to this guy a couple of years later."

"If he didn't tell her about his past—"

"They've got two daughters: Amanda and Diane."

"What beautiful names."

"Very snotsy. Somebody's making up for something they didn't have."

"I don't see how you get that out of it."

"What's wrong with Mary or Jane?"

"Maybe they're names that were in the family, like ours. How old are the little girls?"

"Seventeen and sixteen."

"That's impossible."

"I was a little surprised about that, too."

"They're so close to our age. And they're your sisters, Bruce. Your real sisters."

"As real as real can be. You think your mother's married? Or still single? What do you want to bet? Bet you ten bucks she's got a family."

"It feels really peculiar to imagine it. I'd always thought about her on her own."

"Five bucks?"

"Okay. You know, she was just about my age—a few months older. I can't get over it."

"Didn't you expect that, after I'd been to them?"

"It seems to me," Alma said, "I keep expecting the wrong things, so I'm always caught off balance."

AFTER BRUCE LEFT, Alma made plans. On the next Saturday she took a bus in to the city, where she bought a pair of shoes with part of her birthday money. Then she went to the library, looked at some books in the dance section for a while and, after that, she walked upstairs. In the alcove off the hall between the coffeeshop and the cafeteria, she found the telephones. She looked through the phone books. Just as Bruce had said, there were societies and clubs for adopted children. In fact, there were several. When she called the number listed under *Hotline Trouble,* the woman who answered took a while to come up with any information. Alma could hear her turning pages, minute after minute, until finally the voice came back with four phone numbers, saying, "Sorry it's taken so long. We mostly get calls about drugs or suicide or, uh, that kind of thing."

Alma looked over her shoulder. The corridor leading to the coffeeshop was empty, so was the hallway outside the cafeteria. She dialed the first number on the list. Her request was not the usual one there, either; most people undoubtedly got in touch with such societies in order to talk about their feelings toward both sets of parents—the real and (as Bruce sometimes put it) the unreal.

"Hello," a woman's voice said.

"Oh, hi," Alma answered. "Is this Adop—"

"Yeah. What can I do for you?"

"Well, I just wondered. If I tried to find my real mother, do you think . . ."

"Yes?"

"Do you think it might upset her?"

"I don't know."

Some advice line you are, Alma thought. *I don't know.*

"Nobody can know that," the woman said. "So, don't worry about it. Ask yourself how important it is to you, not to her. Okay?"

"Okay. Thanks," Alma said. She hung up quickly, before anyone could ask her if she wanted to join the society. She felt altogether less confident than before she'd made the call.

During the trip home, she changed her mind. She started to think that the woman on the other end of the line had been right: it was up to her.

BRUCE SENT her a letter that told her everything he'd been able to discover about her mother. After the adoption, Rose E. Parker had gone to Chicago, where she had trained to be a librarian. She'd also taken some courses at a teachers' college. For eighteen months she'd lived with an aunt, then she'd found a job teaching in a small country school in Iowa. She'd stayed there for two years, had taken another job in Washington State, and had met her husband: a man named Thomas Shelton, who was an accountant. After the wedding they'd moved to California and had started to buy a house. They had two children, Jerome and Tobias, aged ten and eight. At the moment, Rose had gone back to teaching. Her husband, Thomas, was working for a large accountancy firm.

Jerome? Alma thought. *And Tobias?* They sounded like the names of old men with beards. She wondered if either Rose or Thomas had joined some kind of religious sect.

She sent Bruce a check for five dollars. And she started to think about all of them—Rose, Thomas, Jerome and Tobias —so frequently that it was like being haunted by the present and the future, rather than by the past.

She began to invent scenes in which she met them. She forced her fantasies to go all different ways: sometimes she'd encounter hostility; once, the mother threw herself at her and demanded that Alma should compensate her for everything else that had gone wrong in her life. In most of her daydreams Alma would remain in hiding. She'd see her mother waiting for a bus or shopping at a supermarket. She'd go up and stand next to her. And that would be enough.

A month before graduation, she talked to Bess about her other family and about the visit to the adoption agency earlier in the year. She didn't mention Bruce's part in the business. If he meant for Bess to know anything, he could tell her himself. Alma never wanted him to feel that she had been disloyal to him over even the smallest thing. He suffered too much already from his obsession about betrayal.

"It's something I've got to settle," she said. "I don't need to talk to her, or to know what she's like or what she thinks, or anything. I just have this sort of craving to see what she looks like. Do you understand?"

"Of course," Bess said. "It's only natural."

"I didn't say anything before, because I didn't know how to put it. You know I'm glad you're both my parents, don't you?"

Bess laughed. She said, "You do just whatever you want to

about it, Alma. The only thing I'd ever worry about is if one of you got hurt."

"Me and this other woman?"

"You or Bruce. You're my family."

"I thought I'd better tell you now, because that's why I'll be going all the way to California. That's where they live."

"Oh," Bess said. "That's a long way. That's a long way, with both of you gone."

After his June exams Bruce asked the college authorities to let him take the next year off, and to be readmitted as a sophomore on his return. He described the need for such a long break as "family affairs." They allowed him the time because he was one of their best students.

He moved to Kentucky. In the summer he started work on a newspaper. He also hired himself out as a gardener.

He saw them. He saw him first—the husband: Raymond. That was a week after he'd flimflammed his way into the newspaper office.

He was supposed to be covering a local fair, for which he had a photographer named Wilbur Spinks in tow. Wilbur wanted to get some shots of horses. And since Bruce was always asking, "Who's that?" or, "Tell me about such-and-such," Wilbur told him, unasked, "Those two over there are Harold Judd and Ray Baxter. Harold's president of the downtown bank."

"I recognize him," Bruce said.

"And Ray's a real good man to know if you ever want a car.

He's got a lot of businesses: stables, electrical supplies. He just bought the old Tropic Club last year—The Tropic Night. It used to be a kind of nightclub. Big business back in prohibition days. Now it's all wired up for disco stuff."

Bruce took a long look at the husband. Baxter was standing with his jacket slung over one shoulder and his shirtsleeves rolled up. He wore a pair of lightly tinted glasses against the sun. His hair was black and gray, his body thickset but not fat. He had the appearance of a man who took good care of himself, but he also seemed like someone who hadn't been born with the expensive jacket and sunglasses and the generally easy air of comfort. He looked tough. You wouldn't want to get into a fight with a man like that.

The wife came later: Joanna Elizabeth. Bruce was writing out a deposit slip at the bank. He heard one of the cashiers say, "Mrs. Baxter." He looked up, seeing her distinctly in three-quarter profile and hearing her voice, although not clearly enough to distinguish the words.

She was as glamorous as a moviestar or a television actress: honey blonde, slim, in a pale knitted suit and strappy, high-heeled shoes. Her face was hard, pretty and bored. She had her sunglasses in one hand, gesticulating with them. The stones in her rings flashed as she moved her hand. She looked young and sexy, and as if she intended to give that impression. The shoulder-length hair had been artificially streaked, her make-up applied in order to attract. The lines of her figure were easily followed through the material of the clothes she wore. You'd never have thought she had two grown daughters. He looked and looked, as if caught in a ball of fire, consumed by the power of his own eyesight. He would have known she was the one, even if he hadn't heard some-one speak her name. *Not two,* he thought: *three. She's had three children.*

ALMA TOOK two training courses over the summer: teaching and librarianship. While she was studying, she met a man named Ernest Allgood. She told him that she'd just been in a play called *The Importance of Being Earnest.* He said: Yes, he had the perfect name for a villain.

He was in his early thirties, divorced, and had a daughter. The wife had remarried. They'd separated within three years. He told Alma that he still liked his wife; she was a nice girl. The trouble was that they'd both been too young for marriage.

Alma was lonely. She missed Bruce all the time. Now that school was over, she felt as if she'd parted from her parents too, even though she still lived with them. Ernest was easy-going and jovial. She didn't want to lose his company, but there was no way of explaining to him that she just needed a friend. He wanted to sleep with her.

He kept her laughing and made her feel comfortable, and one evening got a couple of drinks into her and took her to his place. She kept saying, "Don't get me pregnant," and he kept repeating, "Don't worry. I'm not going to get you preg-nant." She thought afterwards that she'd probably known—before going home with him—how the evening would turn out, otherwise she'd have told him that she didn't want to see him any more.

She went back to Dr. Morse and asked all about birth con-trol. This time she could talk. She even thought of asking how many women who got pregnant wanted to. But it was no use asking a thing like that. In any case, she now believed the answer to be unconnected to medical fact: it was a matter of opinion. All people had their opinions. And sometimes they had other people's on loan, either temporarily or because that was the only way they could acquire any of their own. There were lots of things you couldn't find out by asking other people.

Ernest said to her, "I never knew a girl who was so scared of getting pregnant."

"It's what happened to my mother."

"It's what happens to all mothers."

"I mean my real mother. That's why I'm adopted."

"Oh."

"I never understood how it could have happened if she hadn't wanted it. But now I do. Because I did the same thing. I left it up to the man. When you said everything was all right, I believed you."

"It's true. It's all right."

"It better be."

"What would you do if it wasn't?"

"I'd rather be dead."

"You don't mean that."

She did mean it. She said so.

"Don't you want children?" he asked.

"Sure, but not yet." She had discovered that it was possible to live with someone, without love, as long as you were decent to each other. You could still have a good life. But to have the child of a man you didn't love: that would be different. She wondered if that had been her inheritance—if her mother had carried her so unwillingly that every drop of blood going to the womb had helped to produce a creature that would look for ways to make itself miserable.

For the moment, and as long as she didn't get stuck in her thoughts about love and family, everything was all right. She was happy with Ernest. At the end of the summer he asked her to marry him. She said no. He told her that he'd been a fool to take her to bed so soon: if he'd waited, he'd have been able to win her over.

"I could have had you for life," he said, "instead of just this summer. You aren't really going way out to California, are you?"

They sat in his kitchen: he talked and she drank coffee. He kept reaching over to take her hand. She couldn't understand how it was that she should feel so queasy about breaking off with a man she didn't love as much as she ought to. If she'd loved him better, she wouldn't be feeling so bad. But, of course, if she'd loved him, she wouldn't be going away. He wanted to know if he'd see her again. She said she hoped so. He told her that he should have gotten her pregnant after all. Even if he had, she thought, it wouldn't have done any good. She was still in love with Bruce.

She left for California at the weekend.

SHE'D SPENT hours writing letters. *Dear Mrs. Shelton. Dear Mother. Dear Rose Ellen. Maybe you don't want to hear from me but . . . I hope you don't mind if I ask you a few questions about yourself, just . . . My name is Alma. My mother's name was Rose Ellen Parker. Do you think we could meet sometime, just to say hello?*

She hadn't been able to finish any of them. She'd asked

herself how she'd feel if a letter came to her out of the blue, eighteen years after the event that still must be one of the most dramatic, even if perhaps not the worst, in her life.

Her mother might feel hunted and distressed. She might suspect blackmail, or that Alma was out to pay her back for making her illegitimate. She might hate Alma. Mrs. Roberts had said that Rose Ellen went through a bad time after the birth. *Maybe she'd want to hurt me,* Alma thought. *Maybe she'd think I really put her through it. Maybe she'd tried to get an abortion and couldn't.* The fact that Rose had later had two more children—and so, presumably, had been happy to become a mother again—might not contradict what had gone before. People always had room for all the emotions and they could change their mind at any time.

She didn't believe that she had the right to disturb the life her mother had made for herself. She decided not to say anything—just to get to know her for a little, and then move on.

BRUCE MET the two daughters at a dance. He danced with the older one first. She was called Mandy. The younger one was Didi. He didn't feel for a single minute that there was anything sweet or sisterly about them. They were stuck-up, brainless egoists with rich-kid affectations. He hated them.

He talked Mandy into going out with him later that same night, and Didi the week after. He could have laughed at how easy it was. They practically threw themselves at him.

ALMA SAW her mother, Rose, standing with two boys at the door of the school library. She knew that that was who the woman was. The younger child was looking up and holding out his hand while he talked—as if he might, babylike, tug at her clothing to hold her attention. The mother looked down and spoke. Alma saw with a pang that the woman had some gray hair. Surely she was still too young to start going gray. But perhaps it ran in the family. Maybe she too would go gray early. She felt shy in the presence of the two boys. It amazed her to think that they were her brothers. She wanted to back away.

Rose laughed at something the older boy said, and looked up. She caught sight of Alma. She said, "Hi. Are you here about the Beatrix Potter?"

"I'm here about the job," Alma said. She moved forward. She held out her hand. They introduced themselves. Rose told her the names of the children, Jerry and Toby, who said, "Hi," and ran off. She led the way back into the library. Alma couldn't think of anything except how strange it was that she should be taller than either of her mothers.

A few days later she met the husband, Tom. He walked over to pick up the boys from school. He was working at home that day; their house was only a few blocks away. As he approached, Jerry and Toby were asking Alma to show them how she could do the splits; she'd made a tremendous impression on them by kicking high into the air so that her foot was above her head.

"I'm Tom Shelton," he said. "I guess you're Alma, is that right?"

They stood talking while the boys collected their sneakers and notebooks. Toby had to go back into his classroom to find a box of crayons he'd left behind.

Tom was light-eyed and freckled and had a wiry build. His manner was friendly. He couldn't stand still for long but bounced up and down on his toes or shifted his weight from one foot to the other. He looked younger than his wife. Rose had told Alma that he was at a good stage in his work. When things piled up, he got tense: his stomach would begin to bother him and he'd lose weight.

"They're nice boys," Alma told him.

"Oh, they're great," he said. "But Rose always wanted a daughter."

Was it possible that Rose had never said anything? No. She'd have had to tell her husband. It would be too big a risk if the truth ever came out. And besides, Alma thought, if a man didn't love you enough to want to know that kind of thing about you, there wouldn't be much point in getting married to him, especially after you'd been let down once already.

Rose talked a lot about her family. She didn't chatter— sometimes she wouldn't say anything for a long time. And then she'd tell you something about herself, as if she'd known you for years. *She likes me,* Alma thought.

One day while they were reshelving the nature and biology sections of the library, a floorboard creaked on the upper level, where the gallery was. Rose looked up. She ran her eye around the curve of the balustrade on the second story.

Alma said, "What is it?"

"It's the ghost. It always makes me nervous."

"What ghost?"

"I was in here one day, all alone, and I couldn't stand it. I don't believe in those things at all, but I had to leave."

"What ghost?" Alma said again.

The building they were in, Rose told her, had at one time been a large private house. Late in the last century, at about the turn of the century, the house had been bought by a man from San Francisco, who was newly married to a beautiful young wife. He and the wife had come up from town to move in. They were still on their honeymoon. As soon as they arrived, she started to unpack. She opened one of his suitcases that had a loaded pistol in it and the pistol went off and killed her instantly. Three people connected with the school had seen her ghost, standing up on the balcony in a long, dark dress.

"Do you think it was really an accident?" Alma asked.

"Oh, I'm sure it was. They'd just been married. They were happy. It was a terrible thing."

"It seems funny to pack a loaded pistol like that."

"Everybody carried guns in those days. It wouldn't have been so unusual. And they'd always be loaded, in case you needed to use them."

"When she appears, is she unhappy?"

"No. She's just there. She's drawn to the house."

"You really believe it?"

"I don't know. I only know I wasn't able to stay here when I heard the boards starting to make noises. It went all the way around, like somebody walking."

"My mother used to tell me ghost stories," Alma said.

"But this one is true."

"They're all supposed to be true."

"Do you come from a big family?"

"Just the two of us, me and my brother." Alma went back to the books. She added quickly, "We're both adopted." There was a long pause. She kept her head turned away.

Rose asked, "Do you ever think about your real mother?"

Alma began to feel suffocated. She felt as if she were dying. She said, "Yes, a lot."

60

"Do you hate her?"

"Of course not." She looked up, but Rose had moved; she was staring down at a book in her hand and her voice sounded muffled. "I just knew somebody once," she said, "who told me that that was how a lot of adopted children felt. They hated the real ones for letting them go. So, they never wanted to meet them."

"My brother feels that way. Full of hatred. But he's a man. He isn't ever going to get pregnant and not know what to do."

"But I guess it would be hard to forgive."

"Not for me."

She's going to tell me now, Alma thought. But Rose didn't say anything more: she sighed. She gave her attention to the books. All the science sections, she said, were in a mess.

At the end of the day Alma went back to her room and lay down on the bed. She shut her eyes. The moment had been there and she'd missed it. She thought: *I was the one who should have said something. Why didn't I tell her? I ought to have. But I couldn't. I ought to now. But I can't. That was the time. And I let it go.*

BRUCE HAD the two girls exactly where he wanted them. They were frustrated and baffled. They'd been used to calling the tune. By the time they realized that he was going out with both of them, and each suspected that he might be sleeping with the other, he was entirely in control of the situation. He denied his complicity, while seeming to enjoy the flattery of accusation. He said, "Oh, she's exaggerating. She's making it up. She's jealous. I take her out sometimes because she's your sister. I feel sorry for her. She's sort of got an obsession. She says it feels better to talk about it."

It was like being in a school play again, but doing half a dozen parts at the same time. He had to keep remembering what he'd said to which one.

He was introduced to the parents. Ray made an effort to engage him in conversation about newspaper space and advertising. Joanna looked him up and down and smiled slyly. She flirted with him, though not so openly that her husband could see it. Bruce couldn't make up his mind about whether she'd be an unfaithful wife. He guessed that maybe she would, if she thought she could get away with it, but she might be afraid of her husband. It was possible that Ray too was the type to have somebody else on the side, but if so, it wouldn't be serious; you could see that he was crazy about Joanna. And he was full of plans and schemes and deals that kept him busy. He'd probably never had much time to spare for the daughters; he was proud of the way they both looked, but Bruce didn't think he'd have any idea that they weren't pure as lilies and actually hadn't been that way for a couple of years.

Bruce gave Joanna a sympathetic look as she complained about the state of the garden. He said that if she didn't know what to do about the laurel bushes at the end of the path by the trees, he'd take a look at them: he wasn't an expert, but he'd picked up quite a lot of information while he was working on people's lawns.

"Oh, we have a man for all that," she said dismissively.

"Well, tell him they're dying, then. It isn't just the weather. The boxwood bushes don't look too hot, either, and they're American box, aren't they?"

Her eyebrows rose. She looked utterly disdainful. He didn't

know how he'd offended her, but he had. He'd also made her interested in him, he could tell. So, the other part didn't matter.

He smiled pleasantly and said, "Just a suggestion. It's your garden."

AFTER CLOSING TIME Alma went back to the library to look for a letter that she thought she'd left there. She searched all around the places where she'd been doing the reshelving downstairs, then she walked up to the gallery.

The late afternoon sun threw a pattern of bars down from the upper railings to the stairs she was climbing. Her footsteps echoed in the empty building. She thought how strange sound was: a voice or a step could be soft, yet the effect of it was to touch everything. Even a breath could be heard, if you were listening for it, from one end of a building to the other.

The stairs creaked. When she reached the top, she crossed to the point farthest away from the front door downstairs. From where she stood, she could see the two staircases leading down on either side and, beyond them, the opposite wall like the other half of an egg: built in a curve similar to the one she stood against. All the wall was lined with book-filled shelves, but in front of her and on the right-hand side, windows let the sun in. Motes moved soundlessly along the trails of light. Now that everything had been closed and locked for the night, the atmosphere was becoming slightly stuffy.

She found it hard to imagine what would have been there a century before. Perhaps there had been a ballroom with a balcony. It seemed unlikely that a private gentleman would have made provision for such an extensive library.

She turned to the wall, where she'd been standing earlier in the day. There were the three stray books she'd meant to check and, under them, the letter from Merle. She pulled the letter out from underneath. As she did so, the floorboards at the far end of the gallery began to squeal. She turned around, the letter in her hand. She stared across at the windows.

There was nothing. But the wood continued to make intermittent, small noises. She put the letter into her pocket and waited. She was about to head for the stairs when the sounds changed from single, isolated noises to a pattern. Clusters of tapping came from the floorboards at the opposite end of the oval; they moved in bunches, like spurts of rain.

Arnie Lodz, who taught science to the seventh graders, had a theory about the library and its ghost. Long before he'd been told what he might expect to see, he'd come across an apparition. Naturally, he wasn't discounting the possibility that indirect influence had prepared him. First of all, he'd heard a regular step that sounded like someone walking in high-heeled boots or shoes. At the same time there had been a rustling and swishing sound as of a long skirt in motion. His explanation of the phenomenon cited temperature, displacement of weight, the drop and warp of timbers. He also suspected the proportions of the solid parts of the structure compared with the spaces in between. Everyone who had ever lived in an old house, he said, knew about the noises you could hear at night from the expansion or contraction of the wood.

Arnie had taken measurements in the gallery, had removed samples of wood and plaster, had noted the temperature at different times of the day and night. He'd studied the moisture level and he'd rigged up an apparatus for detecting any airwaves that might be expelled from the walls or floorboards as changes took place within them. In addition to all that, he'd left a sensitive recorder in the building overnight. But none of his researches bore fruit. He'd never figured out where the manifestation—whatever it was—had its source, nor along what lines it proceeded. And he'd never encountered the ghost again. "If it weren't for the fact that I'd actually seen the thing myself," he'd told Alma, "I'd say the origin of it is that people know it's supposed to be there."

Her eye traveled from the windows to the floor and back to the extreme end of the gallery. She waited.

The sounds began again. As before, they started next to the far windows, along the floor: the stepping, the whispering rustle and the patter of little creaks. But this time they seemed to be coordinated, so that as she listened, the uneven bursts fell into a forward-winding scheme almost like something that might issue from a slow, uncertain worker at a typewriter, but more akin to lines of music being tapped out with slight variations at every repeat.

She was about to walk forward to investigate, when it was as if she'd been anticipated: the repetitive snapping and creaking moved from the end of the gallery and began to follow the curve of the bannisters along the right side of the oval. As they approached the place where she stood, they grew louder and faster, hammering. She turned her head to the right. She tried to trace the drumming course of the noise along the railing, but her eye was caught by something above—a movement in the air.

It was in a hurry, coming at her fast, but she couldn't understand what it was; it seemed to be a large smear or a wave or a knot of movement, or as if something had gone wrong with her eyes.

Her mouth opened, her hands gripped the edge of the shelf to her right. The noises came straight up to her, almost to her feet, and as they stopped, the wavelike bundle of smudges unraveled and rolled away into nothing. It was as if the air were coming apart.

The light in the library appeared to settle itself at a lower pitch. Everything looked normal. Whatever it was, had gone. And as soon as she realized that it was over, she knew that what had happened was so strange that it was impossible.

God, she thought, *what was it?* It wasn't a person, so it couldn't have been a ghost. It was like seeing an eclipse, if you didn't know what one was; if you didn't realize that it was natural, you'd be frightened.

But perhaps there wasn't any explanation.

Alma was in the middle of taking the sixth graders through the scrubland behind the science lab, when a senior named Muriel started to shout her name from the paintshop steps. The girls and boys had their notebooks out to write down descriptions of insects and plants; a boy called Roger even brought a magnifying glass with him, although he and his friends were using it to look into each other's noses and ears; before being warned, they'd tried to light a fire with it.

Alma appointed a bossy girl to look after things. She hurried to Muriel, who said that there was a phone call from her father. She ran.

Elton told her that Bess had had a heart attack and had been taken to the hospital: she'd had another, minor one when she arrived there. He wanted Alma to come home. He also wanted to know if she had Bruce's telephone number, because it didn't seem to be anywhere in the house. She told him that she was coming straight away and that she'd call Bruce for him.

She found Rose, who began to organize the taxi, the packing and the money, so that there would be no need for Alma to waste time by going back to her room.

She telephoned Bruce. He answered, but she didn't recognize his voice. "I'd like to speak to Mr. Manson," she said. That was the name he'd chosen for his locked mailbox.

"How did you get this number?" he asked. He hadn't recognized her, either. He sounded furious.

"Bud," she said, "it's Sissy. It's an emergency." She told him about Bess and Elton. She said that he'd be able to get home before she could, even if she caught a flight.

"I can't," he told her.

"You've got to."

"I just can't, Alma. You go, and hold the fort for me."

"She may die."

"If she does, there's nothing I can do about it by being there."

"She's had two heart attacks."

"I've got to go now," he said. "Call me when you get there. Goodbye." He hung up.

She telephoned the airport. There were cancellations because of fog; what flights there were had been delayed. She wouldn't be able to fly direct in any case: all the seats were booked. She'd have to take a bus and try to catch a plane farther along the line. At least she'd be on her way, heading east.

Rose put her into a cab and told her not to worry: the library would be all right, the school would hold her salary. "We'll be thinking of you," she said.

The moment Alma was on the bus, she took a pill to calm herself down. It didn't work; it didn't even get rid of the headache she had, but after an hour she fell asleep. She dreamt that she had a quarrel with Bruce. He was sitting next to her in the bus, telling her that she had to make excuses for him because that was her job. She started to cry with hopelessness and vexation. She told him it was bad enough that he didn't love her, but to force her to lie to somebody he ought to love was worse. He said, "You've got to," and she answered, "I can't." Then he told her, as if in punishment, "I've got to go now," and he disappeared. At that moment the bus swung sideways, crashed and turned over. The windows changed into partly emptied spaces of white granules, like cracked sheets of ice. People screamed and coughed. A thick, dark smoke began to fill the tangled interior, pouring past her and out of the lacy, fragmented windows. Someone tried to climb over her. She hit and kicked, struggling to get ahead, until at last she pulled herself through and fell on to the road. She still had her coat and shoulderbag clutched in one hand.

She ran along the road. All she could think of was that she had to get to the hospital and now she was late. It was like those dreams where you thought you were either going to miss something important, or else you wouldn't be able to stop something terrible from happening: you were afraid, all the time, that you wouldn't get there soon enough.

The roadway was in confusion; cars were stopping and traffic was building up. She saw a police car and ran to it. The driver honked the horn at her. He almost drove into her. Both men inside screwed down their windows and started to shout at her, to get out of the way. She yelled back at them, saying that she had to get to the airport because her mother was in the hospital. "You're blocking the road," the driver told her. She said that if they didn't get her to the airport, she was never, never going to buy another ticket to the policemen's ball and, besides, she'd taken down the number on their license plate. The one in the passenger seat said, "I guess you'd better get in, otherwise Murphy here won't have anybody to dance with this year." He opened the door. She got in. The driver said, "Christ Jesus, Frank." His friend told him, "Have a heart." He explained to her that they had to stay at the scene of the accident, but they'd call another car for her and it would take her to the airport.

She waited. Then she was in the car; and right after that, at the airport. She stood at the counter. Once again, people tried to get in her way. Some of them kept asking her if she was all right. She told everybody about having to get to the hospital. Finally they let her have the boarding pass. The next thing was a scene where she was standing in front of a mirror. Her blouse was ripped and covered in blood and her face was streaked with dirt. Near the hairline, on a level with her ear, she had a small cut that had bled copiously. A woman in a uniform put a bandage over the cut and cleaned the rest of her face. Alma kept jerking away. "I have to get to my mother," she said. She looked into the mirror, where she saw herself getting into the bus that was driving out to the plane. Bruce was still sitting next to her. "Look," he said.

Right in front of them a plane turned sideways and hit the wing of another plane. *Not again,* she thought. The bus swerved and braked. The driver backed up. He drove out on to the grass and stopped. Alma could see ambulances going past. Bruce said again, "I have to go now." She asked, "Why?" "They're coming to take me away," he told her. When she looked, he was gone, just like the other time. She turned back and peered at the window. She was in the plane. The man next to her said, "You're not very talkative." She closed her eyes. The man said, "Not very friendly, are you?"

WHEN SHE LANDED, she telephoned the hospital. The nurse who answered went and got Elton for her. He said to hurry. She went to the head of the line at the cab rank and said she was sorry, but she had to get to the hospital to see her mother. She was crying. The people who were getting in to the next taxi stood back to let her go first, but the ones behind them didn't like having to wait. They began to quarrel. Alma got in. As the driver started up, two of the quarreling people called something after her.

Elton was waiting at the front doors of the hospital. He gave her a hug. At that moment she realized that she wasn't dreaming. She'd been awake ever since the bus had crashed: that was what had woken her up.

"This way," he said. He led her to an elevator and afterwards out into a long corridor. A nurse came towards them. She took Alma by the arm.

They turned off to the left and straight into Bess's room. Alma went up to the side of the bed. She leaned down and touched her mother's face. Bess turned her head on the pillow; she opened her eyes. "Hi, Alma, honey," she said. She swallowed twice.

"I came as fast as I could."

"It sure is nice to see you," Bess said. Her voice wasn't much above a whisper. Alma touched her face again.

Bess sighed. "Did Bruce come with you?" she asked.

"He'll be coming from Kentucky. I was still in California."

"That's right. I forgot. I'm all mixed up."

"Don't worry about it."

A nurse came from behind one of the screens and murmured, "Not too long."

Alma said, "I guess they want you to rest a little."

"Where's Bruce?"

"He'll be here soon," Elton said.

"I couldn't get hold of him," Alma said. "I'll try again, just as soon as I can get to a phone."

Bess smiled groggily. *They've probably given her a lot of drugs,* Alma thought. *Because she's in such pain.*

"Maybe you could phone from here," Elton said.

Alma asked the nurse if she could make a long-distance call. She told her parents, "I'll be right back."

Bruce must have been waiting by the phone because he answered before she expected it, saying, "Yes?"

"Bruce, it's Alma."

"Where are you?"

"Home. At the hospital."

"How is she?"

"Not good. You've got to come."

"I can't, Alma. I can't explain, but I can't come."

"I came. My bus crashed on the highway and I had to climb

over dead bodies to get out, but I did it. This is more important than whatever you're doing. Bruce, if you don't come home now, I'll never forgive you. I mean it. She's asking for you."

He said again that he couldn't. He hung up. She'd forgive him: she'd have to.

She went back along the corridor. Bess had died while she was out of the room. Elton was sitting with his head down on the body, his arms out.

Another dream last night, that I was traveling. Then I arrived at a hotel somewhere in Europe where the people were French-speaking. It might have been Belgium, Switzerland or France. The hotel was a large, fine old place in a spa town. I signed my name in the register at the reception desk, but after I'd done it, the clerk behind the counter said, "And now, will you sign your real name?" I said, "What are you talking about?" And he turned the register around to me again, saying, "We need your real name." I looked at the name I'd written, and realized that it was an alias because I was an espionage agent, working on a case, and it was very important that I shouldn't give my right name. I said, "I lost it at the train station when my wallet was stolen, but I should be able to let you have it in a couple of days." The answer appeared to satisfy him.

AFTER ALMA came home from the hospital with Elton, she made some sandwiches and the two of them watched the news on television. There were pictures of the bus crash she'd been in and the aircraft accident she'd only just missed.

"That was my bus," she said.

"Which?"

"That one there."

"Eight people died."

"That's how I got the cut in front of my ear. And that plane crash: I wasn't in it, but we were right near where it was. We drove by it." She tried to recall scenes from the past day but she couldn't get them in sequence. She sat still, her eyes staring ahead until the program was over.

"I think maybe you ought to get some rest," Elton suggested.

"Just as soon as I make a couple of phone calls."

She telephoned California. Tom answered. He sounded pleased to hear her. He called Rose to the phone.

Rose said, "We were so worried. There was that bus wreck, nearly everybody dead, and then a crash at the airport, too. The boys were going crazy. They kept saying that even if you'd missed one, you might have been in the other one."

Alma told her that she'd been in the bus; and that she'd seen the accident at the airport. She was all right. But her mother had died, so she was going to stay on for a while. She didn't know for how long. It might be a week. Or longer.

She phoned Bruce one more time.

As soon as he picked up the phone, he asked, "What's happened?"

When she told him that Bess was dead, he said he was sorry. She gave him the date Elton had set for the funeral.

He said, "I won't be coming."

"You'd better."

"How would that help her?"

"It would help us. It would specially help Daddy."

"He'll be all right. He's got you there."

"Why did you give me your number, if it wasn't for something like this? What could be worse than this?"

"Jesus, Alma, don't fold up on me now. I gave it to you so you could tell me what was going on."

"Well, I'm telling you. Come on home."

"No, I can't," he said, and hung up again.

After that, she went to pieces. She cried for four minutes without stopping, and then collapsed on the front hall floor. Elton got Dr. Mason over straight away; he told him about Bess's death, the bus crash, everything. Dr. Mason said it was possible that Alma was suffering from delayed shock, but as far as he could tell at the moment, she was actually just asleep.

They carried her up to her room, took off her shoes and put a blanket over her. Elton asked the doctor to stay and have a drink. Dr. Mason looked at his watch and said: Yes, sure, there was time for a beer. They sat and talked for twenty minutes or so.

I dreamt that I was getting married to Alma. We were standing in front of the preacher and he said, "Do you, Bruce," and so on. And I said, "I don't have to. We're already married." And then I remembered that we'd been married for about two years. Alma said, "That's right. We're just doing it to get the piece of paper." We went through the ceremony and, at the end, a man in an usher's uniform came out of a back room and handed Alma a piece of paper that was just that: a tiny, little torn scrap about an inch long. But she seemed very happy with it. She put it down the front of her dress to keep it safe.

ALMA SLEPT for fifteen hours. When she woke up, she remembered seeing blood and smoke, hearing children screaming. She saw the faces of the people she'd hit and kicked in order to get out of the bus first. In order to get to the mother who wasn't her true mother, she'd been willing to kill innocent people, who were in the same trouble she was in. And when she'd managed to fight her way home, she'd found out that her mother was only really interested in seeing Bruce.

But that was the way it had always been. She shouldn't be disappointed or surprised any longer. She should accept things. She closed her eyes, but didn't sleep. She was busy thinking. She thought and thought, and couldn't remember what she was supposed to be thinking about. After a while she got up and went downstairs.

Elton met her at the foot of the stairs. He didn't want to talk about the future, or even about the past. He had a cousin who could come visit him; and Bess had a widowed sister-in-law. There were other cousins, too.

"I'll stay as long as you like," she offered. "It's only a job. I told them a week, just to let them know I'd be away."

"A week is fine."

"I don't have to go back to California at all."

"I appreciate it, Alma. But I'd like to be alone for a while. To get things straight in my mind. Do some thinking."

"Who's going to cook for you?"

"Oh, I can handle that. Maybe if you could do some of the packing up—clothes, and that kind of thing."

"Of course."

"It's hit me pretty hard," he said.

I was in the hospital and Alma was with me. She was holding my hand. I'd just had one operation, but they were going to do a second one.

I said, "I miss my fiddle. I'd like to hear somebody right now, playing 'Hearts and Flowers' as I go down the drain."

Alma said, "You aren't going to get out of things so easy."

I said, "I'm dying."

"Oh, I don't think so," she told me. "Modern medicine is pretty good. You've got plenty of years left."

"Jesus, I hope not," I said.

They wheeled me away, into the operating theater. Blood filled my lungs, my throat, my mouth. The doctor looked down at me and said, "It's the tide of history."

The nurse standing next to him asked, "Is it twenty to, or twenty past? They go out with the tide, like ships. The moon causes it. It sets the cycle of blood in women. It controls conception, birth, madness and death. It's the heavenly body of lunatics. How can we hope to rule the world when the most important influences in our lives are faceless, nameless, hidden?"

The doctor said, "There's no way to stop the bleeding."

I wanted to see Alma. "Where is she?" I asked them. "I want Alma." But nobody could hear me.

ON THE PLANE to California Alma wrote three letters. The first was to Merle. The second was to the state police, to thank the two officers who had helped her. She'd found their names, with the number of their patrol car, in the notebook she carried in her shoulderbag. She still had no memory of writing down anything during her journey to the hospital. In a p.s. she said that she'd been asleep when the bus accident had happened, and that she'd been in shock when she saw the plane crash at the airport, but if they wanted to ask her any questions about what she remembered, they could find her at the school where she worked.

The third letter was supposed to be for Bruce, but she couldn't finish the first sentence. After a while she came to the conclusion that it would be no use trying to say anything; she was too angry. She thought: *What was so important that you couldn't come to your own mother's funeral? What have you done to your father by staying away? And what have you done to yourself? There's no way you can get back that time and do it over. That was your time and you refused it.*

She slept. She ate part of the airline meal. When the lights were turned down, she got out her pad of paper again. She wrote to Bruce. She described to him the crash she'd been in. She said that it could have been some other kind of disaster—not a catastrophe that threatened physical danger and death, but an emotional calamity. It might not have had to harm her in any way, simply to make her think. *The way I feel,* she wrote, *is that I've survived and that it isn't worthwhile or right to hang on to petty things. I don't think you should nurse a sense of injury and vengeance against these other people. It can't be good for you to be tormenting yourself so. It's hurting you much more than you'll ever be able to hurt them. Let it go. Let people live their own lives and forget what you think they did to you. I won't say anything else about not coming home for the funeral, except that it's important for people to participate in death when it's a death in the family. Dad and I are very sad and grieving, but that's part of it. She's with us and she's gone. But what's happening in your heart? You know I love you. We all love you. Why don't you love anybody back? Couldn't you go home and stay with Dad for a while? And then come to California—or I can come to you. I feel like we could lose each other.*

She mailed the letters as soon as she landed. Bruce answered quickly: he must have written the moment he got the letter. *Don't worry about losing me,* he told her. *Of course I love you back. I'll go see Dad when all this business is finished and then I'll come see you.* He'd crossed out a sentence that had begun *Maybe we can,* and another that had started out *As soon as I'm free of,* and below that he'd just written the word "love" and signed his name.

We can shape history to a certain extent. The course of it follows a pattern of the human mind—or maybe it's just that we think it does because that's how we interpret events.

Even though some causes or ideals seem wrong to us, as far as history is concerned, the right one is the one that wins. Victory is only for a while, anyway. Everything could all come back: the Dark Ages, the wars for a hundred years. If you've got a chance of winning, isn't it better to fight for a hundred years, rather than go under?

ROSE WAS careful not to ask Alma too many direct questions. She asked around the edges: was there someone to look after Alma's father, would she need to take a break to go home again fairly soon, could any of them do anything? No, Alma answered; everything was fine. The two boys, Jerry and Toby, broke the ice: they wanted to hear all about the bus crash. They wanted to see Alma's cut, which had almost healed. Their interest in the scope of the death and mutilations was intense and ghoulish. She was amused, but she told them something of what it had really been like. She didn't include too many details; despite his pleading for gory incident, Toby still had nightmares after seeing monster movies.

Alma thought that she was getting over it; that she was easing herself back into a routine again. But one afternoon in the library, when the two of them were alone at the desk, Rose said something about a mother being a real mother even if, as Alma had told her, she was adopted; and Alma began to cry.

"That's just it," she sobbed. "He didn't come. He wouldn't even come to her funeral. He wanted us to make this pact a long time ago: about how we'd go to the adoption agency to find out about our real parents and then we'd hunt them down. He wanted to get back at them some way. But I never felt like that. I figured it was better to forget everything and just think how lucky we were to be here at all and have a good mother and father: even if we were adopted and they weren't the real ones. He wouldn't even come to her funeral. She was the only mother we had all our lives. And she loved us, even though she wasn't my real mother." She stopped, to catch her breath. She wiped her hands across her face. Rose put her arm around her and patted her back.

Alma got out a Kleenex. She blew her nose. She took a deep breath. "You're my real mother," she said. "That's why I came out here. That's why I got this job. I wanted to see you."

"Oh," Rose said. "My goodness." She looked at Alma as if

trying to recognize someone who was standing a long way off. "Oh," she said again. Her eyes filled with tears.

Alma steered her into a chair. "Let me go get you a glass of water," she said. But Rose caught hold of her hand and wouldn't release it. Alma pulled up a second chair. She sat down. "I wasn't going to tell you," she said. "I thought it might upset you. I shouldn't have said anything."

"It's my dream come true. I've just been thinking about you for too long. My little girl. Do you have another one of those Kleenexes? I've thought about this moment so many times."

"Me, too," Alma said. She pulled a Kleenex out of her pocket and handed it to Rose.

History is only what other people say about you after you're dead, or—if you're lucky—what you get to say about yourself, as long as you're holding the reins. None of it matters at the time, only afterwards.

OVER THE NEXT few days Rose began to tell Alma about her own parents, about her highschool boyfriend and his family: they all still lived in the same town; she'd even seen him again. For a long time she'd hated him, but she'd come to realize that he'd just been young, as she had been. He had a family himself now and she felt nothing against him, or for him. She still couldn't forgive her parents. That was another reason why Tom and the boys meant so much to her. Tom knew the whole story; she'd told him before they were married.

Alma asked all the questions she'd been storing up for years.

"Right at the beginning," Rose said, "I was horrified. I couldn't believe it had happened. I wanted so much for it not to be true. I thought of getting rid of it, I really did. If I'd known a little more, I'm sure I would have. But I didn't know what to do. I told him and he told his parents, and they told mine, and they all got together. I still feel bitter about that, to this day. That's why I don't have much to do with my family any more. They were trying to do their best for me. They said so. I've just never been able to believe that again, not completely. Maybe they wanted to think that was true at the time. It's hard to face the disapproval of a whole town. I wouldn't want to, myself. But if it was a question of my child's future or the town's opinion, I'd get up and go. If I could. I guess it was my father who decided that they couldn't. Anyway, I'm sorry I never met your mother. I could have. When it was getting near the time of the birth, I wanted to. And the agency said it would be all right. But my parents wouldn't allow it. They were afraid of it coming back on them later in some way."

"I wish you'd met her," Alma said.

"So do I. I really do. But you can tell me about her. Did she name you after a relative in her family?"

"Yes. One of her grandmothers."

"It's strange to think of you being called Alma. I never knew anybody named Alma."

"You had another name for me."

"Yes. It was—"

"Don't tell me what it was. Please. I'm the way I am now. I can't be somebody else."

"No, of course. You're right."

"You could meet my father."

"If he'd like to."

"Good. I'll talk to him about it."

They went for a long walk together late one afternoon while the boys were playing over at a neighbor's house. Alma said, "I think it's inhuman that they never let you see me."

"It wasn't the society's policy in those days. Maybe it still isn't. They didn't want the mothers to change their minds. They thought it was better to knock you out in the delivery room and then you'd come to, and all the problems would be over. Everyone was very nice to me. They made me feel as if they thought that there had been a mistake, but it wasn't my fault, and that if I went along with all their advice, I'd be proving how sensible I was; how much character I had. They hardly mentioned the baby once. They just kept saying that there was nothing to worry about. They did tell me it was a girl, that's all. One of the nurses told me; I don't think she was supposed to: she let it slip. You know, while I was carrying you, before I even knew if I was going to have a girl or a boy—I was so mixed up about everything. Sometimes I hated it. Sometimes I had this feeling of hope, of buoyancy—I didn't know what it was: like happiness. It was only later, about ten days after the birth, that I knew how much I loved you. I tried everything to get you back. They told me I'd change. They said it was part of the reaction and I'd get over it. But I didn't. I got worse. I was desperate. They gave me pills and they told me that I had to think about the future: I should ask myself if I wanted it to go down on my record that I was unstable. I might never be able to get a job. So I gave up writing the letters and making the phone calls. I think my mother started to have a bad conscience about me then. But it was too late. I felt that something had been done to me that could never be put right, ever."

"And now I'm here," Alma said.

"All grown up."

"We'll settle down with it. We like each other already, so it'll be all right."

"What if you hadn't liked me?"

"I don't know," Alma said. "I think I'd just have moved on in a couple of weeks."

"It frightens me to think of it."

"I bet it happens. There must be a lot of kids who get a summer job someplace, to look at their parents, and that's all they want to do, whether they like them or not: they just take that one look and go away. That's what Bruce should do."

"Tell me some more about him."

"I wouldn't know where to begin. I hope you'll meet him, too, some day. Then you can see for yourself."

"It's hard to describe people."

"It gets harder, the closer you are to them."

"I've got some pictures from my highschool days. Everything's in a box. I haven't opened it since the adoption. I used to think about throwing it all away, but I never did. There's a photograph of Jim. Do you know something: when we were at school, he was a very good athlete but what he was really wonderful at was—he was the most beautiful dancer you ever saw. I guess that's something you inherited from him."

Alma thought about a teenage boy, a marvelous dancer and younger than she was now. He was no longer anonymous. Something that was hers had once belonged to him, too. There was a way in which he and she were the same.

Now that she knew, she couldn't forget it. She saw a time coming when curiosity would draw her to the place where he lived, not to meet him but just to catch sight of him for an instant.

At the moment, she didn't want to. From having no relatives, she'd gone to having too many. They were beginning to confuse her. She needed to sit down for a long talk with Bruce.

Joanna telephoned him early in the morning. The call came through on his second phone. He'd decided only the day before that he'd give her a ring himself that afternoon.

She said that she was afraid he'd been right about those laurel bushes, and most of the other things in the garden as well: could he come over tomorrow afternoon and talk about it? The girls would both be away on the school glee club weekend. And her husband was going to be looking at somebody's horses all day long. "So, we'll have plenty of time to talk," she told him. "About the garden." Her voice sounded low and purring, as if she'd be smiling. He said: Sure, he'd see her around two-thirty.

That night he went to a movie theater and sat through a double feature. One film was a low-budget light comedy about insurance fraud investigators; it starred a TV actress he liked. The second told the story of a city cop who tried to buck the system, was thrown out of the force and ended up saving the whole of New York single-handed, after shooting thirty-six people.

When he got home he wasn't sleepy. He took a walk.

Back in his highschool years he used to enjoy walking around alone at night in the late spring and early summer; he'd be feeling restless and he'd start out fairly fast, but as the light went he'd calm down until he was moving lazily from street to street, the trees around him growing massive and shaggy with darkness. He used to love walking all through the night. That was another town of white picket fences and neat lawns. At one time he'd detested everything about it. Now he thought of it with the longing of homesickness, and of his youth and childhood that were over forever.

He walked for hours. He tried not to think ahead, not to plan; just to walk from one shadow to the next.

HE GOT the afternoon off by doing a deal with a man at work. He'd arranged it the day before, so he had nothing hanging over him. Everything was going smoothly.

He took his time getting to the house, parked, and sat in the car for a while. The trees were only just beginning to turn. The blue sky had a few bright, puffy clouds in it; the air was mild and stirred by the constant movement of small breezes. He wanted to relax into the beauty of what he was looking at, but instead of giving him rest, the loveliness of the day excited him. Everything he looked at seemed invested with immense significance. He wondered if the strange heightening of emotion—apparent in the world outside as well as within him—meant that he was going to end up killing her.

When he tried to think ahead, it was as if he'd gone blind: as if his mind had entered a kind of night. Things distant and near were equally incomprehensible to him, as were the past and the future, the home that was gone and the one that had never been. He thought that he might have come to the end of his life. He didn't know what he was going to do. He seemed to have forgotten his way.

He knew that the solution to everything would come to him at the right moment, but he ought to have had a plan. What he'd imagined at the beginning was that he'd start with the two daughters. But they'd been too experienced to be damaged, too shallow to be hurt. All he'd done was to prove that they were worthless, and he'd already known that. They had cheated him of his revenge. They were fighting and full of spite against each other, but that wasn't enough. He had to do something to Joanna herself. Maybe he could cause a break between her and her husband. Or—more than that; he might be able to persuade her to run away with him. That would be best of all.

This was the day for it: the culmination. Everything was going to work. Maybe he still didn't know how, but that wasn't important.

He got out of the car and walked down the street to the house. She opened the door before he had a chance to ring the bell. She had a glass in her hand. She smiled as if posing for a photograph, and said, "Hi. Come on in. Have a drink."

"Fine," he said.

She swished away in front of him, across the hall, down two steps, over the living-room rug and to the screened-in porch that looked out on to the garden.

The sliding glass doors were closed; no one would be able to hear them from across the lawn. And the slatted bamboo blinds were drawn on two sides: without a good pair of field glasses, nobody could see them, either. She'd set everything up. All he had to do was to let her fall into it.

She was wearing a silky, wrap-around dress that had appeared to be flowing like water while she walked. Now that she was stretched out on one of the sofas, the material pulled tight so that he could see the lines of a tiny pair of bikini pants underneath and, above the belt at her waist, the shape of her breasts and nipples almost as exactly as if she'd been naked.

"What can I offer you?" she said, in the same voice she'd used over the telephone.

Right, he thought. *I'll make you work for it.* "How about a gin and tonic to start with?"

She got up, mixed him a drink, bent over his chair to hand it to him, dumped some more bourbon into her own glass and repositioned herself on the sofa. She'd made sure that he'd been able to see down her dress. This wasn't going to be the day to examine the shrubs for mildew and leaf rot.

She said, "Why don't you bring that erection over here and let it say hello?"

"I might," he said. He lifted his glass and swirled the ice cubes around. "Why don't you tell me something about yourself first?"

"Like what?"

"Oh, your unspoiled girlhood, how you ended up with a man who's got a jail record—that kind of thing."

"How do you know about that?"

"If you work on a paper, you've got access to a lot of information. I was curious about you."

"Why?"

"Why not?"

"My two girls are both crazy about you."

"Oh?"

"I guess you think you know a lot about girls."

"Uh-huh. And you know about men. So that makes us even."

She moved her leg. Her dress fell open at the side, showing her thigh nearly up to the hipbone.

"Tell me about yourself," he said. "Where did you grow up?"

"In a small town. Full of small people with small minds." She drained her glass and banged it down on the table next to her.

"A lot of them live in big towns too, and in the suburbs."

"But you can get away from them easier there. This town I grew up in—if you were seen talking with somebody on the way home from school, five people would have mentioned it to your mother before you got in the door. That's how I met Ray. He was working on the road. I was on my way to the bus stop. Nobody else used to walk that route; all the girls in my grade were like their mothers—they'd disassociated themselves from me because I'd been out with a boy in the senior class who had a bad reputation. They were all saying I'd been sleeping with him, which I had, of course. You bet your boots. And didn't they wish they had, too. He was the real McCoy, all right. He had what it takes." She reached for her glass, tried to drink from it and realized that it was empty.

Bruce stood up and took the glass from her. He poured her a drink of water with a fistful of ice cubes in it. As he put some more tonic into his own glass, he said, "Go on."

"Sure. I thought he was pretty cute. He's gotten a little beefy now, but you should have seen him when he was twenty-five—Jesus. A little like you, matter of fact, but darker. It was early spring. We had a freak heat-wave. He'd be there with his shirt off and they'd call things out to me—

not the usual dirty stuff: jokes, to make me laugh. It was mainly him. I got to doing it back, just for fun."

He gave her the drink of water, pulled his chair nearer and sat down again. He didn't want to get too drunk to see the right moment when it came. He wanted the news of who he was to be devastating. She was pretending to be drunker than she was; she'd be able to take it in when he told her. "Go on," he said.

"Then one day he waited around the corner for me. Asked me out. So I said yes, and from then on we were just screwing each other to death. You can't imagine what he was like. Me, too. I needed it all the time. When you're that age, it's like being insane. All the time."

"And then?"

"They found out about it, of course. Big scenes. Lower-class thug and how could I demean myself and so on: I was doing it to shock, I didn't really have any interest in him, so on, so forth, trying to make him look bad. I thought I was supposed to have a whiskey here. What is this—gin?"

"It's a light whiskey."

"Brucie, this is so light, it could pass for white in Alabama. Put something in it."

"So what happened?"

"I thought I was so smart. We both did. You know how the legal age for marriage varies from state to state? In Arkansas it's something like fourteen for the girl and sixteen for the boy, but if you've got your parents' consent, it's about twelve and fourteen. South Carolina, too. I think so."

"That was supposed to be the Church's answer to the illegitimacy rate: if you let them get married young, at least all the children would be legal."

"I thought if I got pregnant, they couldn't object. I got a copy of my birth certificate and just waited. Where's that drink?"

"Him?" he said, suddenly understanding. "It was the same guy you're married to?"

"What about that drink, bartender?"

He took her glass, poured out more water and handed it to her. As he sat back down in the chair, his hand brushed against her bare leg.

"So, what happened?"

"Pretty dumb. I'd underestimated how much they hated me. Some parents do. They're forced to have kids because of the social conventions—it's something they need, like a car or a house, to show they've made it. But they don't want them. Maybe I was doing it back, too. Anyway, I waited for it to show, and then they laid it on the line: I was no better than a whore, my moral behavior reflected on them, but I was underage and they were in charge of me and if I didn't agree to have the baby adopted, they'd call the police and have Ray arrested for statutory rape. That's what they can do to a man who screws around with a girl who's—"

"Under eighteen, I know. You should have gotten to the next state before you broke the law."

"Oh, what I should have done. They'd have caught us under the Mann Act, or something else. You can't win against people like that. They'd locked me in my room. I wanted that baby so bad. I couldn't believe they'd be able to do it to me. I figured, if I could just get away, get to Ray, I could give birth by myself and it would be okay. I looked old enough, so we could pass for man and wife. I—" She sat up, with her hands to her cheeks.

"Yes?" he said. He thought she was going to choke, but she started to cry, and to scream, and to shout the rest of her story.

"Those bastards," she shrieked. "Doing that to their own child. Took me in to that adoption place and I fought all the way. Told me how many years he could get behind bars if I didn't cooperate. Till finally, I gave in. I thought—well, we could get married in two and a half years—in a lot of states. And then we could sue, get the baby back, and it would be better than him going to jail. The other girls sitting there in the waiting room—my God. I can still remember them: Cheryl and Pat. Cheryl was engaged to a boy who was just making his way up the office ladder; they were supposed to have their wedding the next April. But his parents and her parents decided that a baby just then would come at the wrong time for everybody. And Pat—she'd had one boyfriend who'd run out on her and another one that said he'd marry her if she got rid of the baby the first one left her with. I really wonder how that place could have pretended it was helping people. I know what they were doing: they were selling merchandise. They got me into their operating theater and I fought. Everybody was screaming, including me. All those papers they have on their walls, to say how they'll heal the sick and be as good as Jesus Christ—you should have seen the whole gang of them on top of me, sticking their needles into me like I was a pincushion. When I woke up, it was all over. The baby was gone. They were nice enough to tell me it was a boy; that was the only decent thing they did: imagine going through all that, and never even knowing? Anyway, I was too weak to put up much resistance afterwards. I kept passing out and crying. My parents got the doctors to tell me that if I didn't pull myself together, I'd be in the hands of the psychiatrists for the rest of my life. I could even be committed. You know, if you've got the money, you can buy a doctor like anything else. That's what they were afraid of, see—that Ray was after their money. My mother kept saying, 'You're doing it on purpose, I know you are.' I guess she was scared people would find out how they'd treated me. I was on the edge of going crazy: I could feel it right next to me. And I was scared, too. But I finally reached a point where I could think. It was like being one step away, and if you got too near, you'd be standing in the shadow. I knew that if I could get my health back, and just keep living, in a couple of years I'd be in the clear: I'd be with Ray, and we'd get the baby back, and we'd have a lot of others, too. It was a good thing I didn't find out till later what they'd really done. They'd had him arrested, of course. He was there in jail, all the time, paying his debt to society. Nice, huh?"

"Perfect. How did you get back at them?"

"I used to think about that a lot. It started to take me over. I couldn't think about anything else. I had less and less of my own life left: they covered everything. Then he got out of jail. He said to forget it; we'd just leave and get married and start our family." She sniffed. He handed her his handkerchief. She said, "You know, it's funny: in a way they were right. I mean, I love him, but he's kind of a lunkhead. And I don't even know if he's always on the right side of the law. We don't have anything in common. Honest to God, I'm lonely as hell sometimes." She started to sob again. She sat up from the sofa, tried to pour out some bourbon and sloshed it over the table and floor. She fell on top of him. He grabbed her around the waist, to keep her from sliding to the floor. She tried to kiss him. Then she tried to hit him in the face. She yelled, "For Christ's sake, are you going to sit there all day like a store dummy? Aren't you going to take me to bed?"

He got a firm grip on her and stood up, holding her in his arms. The chair fell over backwards behind him. The glass slipped out of his left hand on to the floor, and broke. He said, "Okay."

He carried her out of the porch, through the living room and into the hallway. He knew where all the rooms were. It would have been best, and appropriate, to take her to the room she and Ray slept in, but that was upstairs and too far away. He lugged her towards one of the downstairs guest rooms and lurched across the threshold with her.

He almost stumbled, hitting the door with the side of his arm. "Whoops," she cried gaily. He left the door open. It didn't matter; there was no one else at home. As he turned around to drop her on top of the bedspread, her wrist caught the lamp on the night table and knocked it over with a crash.

She was out of her dress in seconds, tugging at his clothes. Twenty minutes later they were still making love when Ray ran into the room and started to shout at them. They turned and broke apart.

Ray was looking at them down the barrel of a shotgun. He fired at Bruce, who fell—deafened, blinded and bleeding—down the side of the bed. Joanna screamed at him to stop, but Ray pulled the trigger again. The blast shot half her face away.

Bruce clenched his jaws against the pain, trying not to make a noise. His hands clutched the blankets down on the floor. Everything was wet. Everything smelled like blood. He heard Ray cursing, and another cartridge going into the barrel. He tried not to breathe. But he had no reason to be afraid:

Ray turned the gun around, put the barrel into his mouth and blew the top of his head off.

It took Bruce several minutes to crawl to the telephone. He was sure, all the way, that he'd bleed to death before he got there.

IT MADE the papers in a big way. The county hadn't had such a crime of passion for years. The two daughters came back from their school trip to find both parents dead, their lover in the hospital and the police telling them that he'd been discovered in bed with their mother.

The younger girl, Didi, slashed her wrists but, being ignorant about the correct method, only managed to make two shallow cuts with a breadknife across the backs of her hands, which she then held up dramatically, declaring that she wanted to die, and look: she'd cut her wrists. Her older sister, Mandy, had more intelligence. She loaded one of her father's pistols and went to the hospital, gunning for Bruce. The policeman on duty there stopped her before she got to his room. The nurses gave her a sedative.

The sheriff himself arrived to ask Bruce for his story. It was one of those things, Bruce told him weakly: they'd started drinking heavily and before they knew it, they were in bed and her husband was standing in the doorway.

Alma came to see him. She sat in the chair and held his hand. His voice was faint and he spoke slowly, but he kept her fingers in a tight grip. "So many transfusions," he said. "Blood. The source of all my troubles. I keep bleeding and they keep pouring it into me. Comes in those jars. Looks dark. Looks brown, like my dream. Could be mud."

"I'm sorry you were shot," she told him, "but I'm not sorry you've got the time to think. Something had to stop you."

"I guess. Didn't stop me soon enough. I was in bed with her."

She said, "I'm glad Mom isn't alive." She could see as she raised her eyes that it was the only thing anyone had ever said—except perhaps the news of his adoption—that had hurt him. "How could you do such a thing?"

"Well," he said, "I felt sorry for her." He looked away and yawned, as if bored. "It seemed like the natural thing to do. She'd been through so much. What her parents did to her: nobody has the right. They took everything away from her at the beginning. Then she fought her way through, and found out she didn't have a very good marriage, after all. I think she started to drink when she realized she didn't love him any more, so it had all been for nothing. She kept talking about her lost child. Well, I just couldn't tell her. I couldn't say: *I'm it and I've been screwing both of your daughters.* Could I?"

"The daughters?"

"Nothing special. Neither was she. Except at the end, of course. That was pretty special."

"I think they want to give you some more blood," Alma said.

"Don't go."

"It's all right," one of the nurses told her. "You can stay."

"Violent man," Bruce whispered. "That's what he was like. Maybe that's what I'm like, too."

"Don't make excuses for yourself."

"Why not? It's true what you said. I've destroyed myself."

"And a lot of other people."

"Yes," he admitted. He turned his face to the side, looking towards the door. She thought that his mind had wandered to something else, but after a while he came back to the subject. He said, "But they don't matter."

"Don't you feel any sorrow for them?"

He caught his breath and swallowed in a way that reminded her of when she'd seen Bess for the last time. "Isn't this enough?" he said.

The nurses began to wheel a table into the room.

"I'm the one you should have slept with," she said.

"Brother and sister?"

"Not by blood."

"Psychologically."

"So much the better. In spite of everything, we're your real family. The others are still nothing to you." She wanted to say he should have been able to figure that out a long time ago. But he looked too tired and he'd never been able to stand criticism. "Try and get well," she told him. "You're the only one I can't spare."

"You always loved me, Alma."

"Always. And if you hadn't been so scared of it, we'd have been all right."

"Think so?" he said.

The nurses advanced with their bottles and jars and rubber tubing. His eyes dilated. He held her hand tightly.

Alma said, "I had a dream about you. And in the dream, you lived."

"I wouldn't bank on it. I just saw the doctor walk down the hall. Same son of a bitch that did the other operation on me: the one that didn't work. Why don't they let me die?"

Alma said, "Stop talking like that. You aren't going to die.

I'll be thinking of you every minute you're in there. I'll be praying so hard, helping you. You're going to pull through just fine. And then you'll get well."

A nurse came up to the bed, saying, "Miss—"

Alma wouldn't pay attention to her. She leaned forward, to catch what Bruce was trying to tell her.

I had a dream that I was in the hospital and Alma came to see me. My time was running out. I could feel it trickling away from me, all my time.

She said, "You aren't going to get out of this so easy. You're going to keep on living."

I was so tired that I wanted to sleep. They were going to do an operation on me. I thought I might sleep through that, too.

A nurse came into the room. Alma said, "I'm not leaving," but I said to her, just like the tough guys in the movies, "Kiss me goodbye, Alma."

She kissed me on the cheek. And I said, "Not like that. That's for strangers." So she kissed me again.

BE MY GUEST

Sandra and her boyfriend, Bert, worked for the same firm. She knew that that was a mistake. She'd known it from the beginning, but mixing business with pleasure was something everybody did. It was just because everyone did it that there were so many warnings against it. Where she and Bert worked, everybody certainly did it all the time. It was convenient. Of course, it was more convenient for people who were married, especially for the men. Bert wasn't married, but somehow he acted as if he were—as if he had other commitments that she didn't have the right to question him about.

On Thursday night they had a quarrel because, having planned—and promised—to take her on a weekend trip, he'd changed his mind and decided to go fishing or hunting, or something like that. He said that he'd be with three other men he'd known from college days. She didn't believe that, or at least she said she didn't, because she didn't want him to break his word to her. If he were really going to trade in a weekend with her for one that meant getting drunk and swapping stories with the boys, then that showed just what he thought she was worth.

On Friday morning she waited to see if he'd back down and tell her that he wanted to be with her, after all. He didn't. He took the flightbag and the smaller tan suitcase and he went off to work, without another word to her, as if she'd agreed to it the night before and as if she hadn't told him, "If you do, I'll know how much you care about me." Why had she said that? It made the outcome seem inevitable. She could have waited, quietly, to see what would happen. But anyway, what she'd said only made the matter appear final for her, not for him. He wouldn't give it a thought. Maybe she'd better spend the weekend mulling over how much it really did matter to her whether he cared, and—if he did or didn't—whether she ought to get out of the affair. Perhaps she should do another kind of thing everyone else did, too: let things slide and start going out with somebody else on the side.

When she got home from the office in the evening, she didn't want to do the laundry or get into the bathtub: Bert might telephone. She walked back and forth, willing the phone to ring, until she couldn't stand the tension. She made herself a cup of coffee, sat down in the easy chair and turned on the television.

She watched a comedy serial, two short westerns and an old black-and-white movie from the thirties. She was thinking of switching the set off when a second film followed—a romantic adventure, shot in lush color and set on a tropical island. From the instant the music began, you could tell what kind of story it would be: just her kind. She burrowed more comfortably into the chair.

At first the film presented a map of the South Seas. Then the printed names and numbers faded, turning into a real picture: a boat, off in the distance. Meanwhile, a mysterious-sounding voice said, *Legend tells us that among the atolls of these vast, uncharted seas there lies an island named Mona Zima, the place of the jewel. So potent is the lure of its fame that, though none return from the quest, it continues to draw to it men of passion and daring. Such a one was Joshua Bridgewater in the year 1908.* At last, young Captain Bridgewater himself was shown, standing masterfully at the wheel of his ship, *The Dauntless,* while the ocean grew stormy. His men came up to ask him questions and he barked back orders. The sea became wild and tumultuous. Sandra took two large gulps of coffee.

As the captain's plight became steadily more dangerous, the voice went on to tell the story: One of the volcanic islands in a little-known and as yet unmapped chain was populated by members of a secret religious cult. Its worshipers sacrificed to an idol that was inlaid with many jewels, all set around one fabulous diamond: an enormous stone (bigger than a fist) of perfect purity. It would have made more sense for the inhabitants of a tropical island to revere a giant pearl and not a diamond, but that was explained; the jewel had been brought to the place by an Indian prince, who was fleeing from his brother's army. Just as the maharajah's ships reached the treacherous reefs, a storm blew up and the seas pounded everything to splinters. All the people were drowned. Nothing survived but a small, ornamental casket that was shaped like a boat and therefore, captainless, floated into calmer waters until it gained the shore. Inside was the diamond. From the moment of its arrival it was considered sacred, not simply on account of its great beauty, but because of the seemingly magical way it had steered itself—as if by conscious will—to a place of safety.

The cult worshipers thought that the large and still-active volcano on their island could be pacified by the light of the jewel. They also believed that the diamond would bring them good luck in general, that they were meant to guard and protect it and that all strangers wished to steal it. Any foreigner who expressed interest in it was told that it didn't exist: it was just a story. If he managed to discover the idol and see it for himself, he was killed.

Captain Bridgewater had started out as a freebooter, but his travels had changed him. He'd been moderately chastened by his ordeal in the storm, although through the exercise of his superb seamanship he'd managed to save his vessel. And as soon as he landed on the island—as the sole survivor of his ship's company—he became a better man: he fell in love. The girl who won his heart was a curvaceous strawberry blonde: she caught his eye as she was about to be sacrificed to the idol. The diamond—so she told him haltingly, in her newly learned English—was angry. It had to be appeased. She had been chosen for the job on the basis of her unusual appearance and perhaps also because her parents had been foreign; they had died many years ago when she was still a baby. No one would tell her how they met their fate, but she guessed that the jewel had claimed them. She herself had never been persecuted. She'd been treated as an honored guest. Now she wondered if, all along, the priesthood hadn't been saving her for this moment.

As soon as the commercials began again, Sandra ran to the bathroom and then to the kitchen. There wasn't time to make another cup of coffee. She settled for a glass of water. She sipped slowly as the movie continued.

The hero, as she might have suspected, was captured. But, since he'd done a good deed earlier in the story when he'd rescued two men from execution, he had helpers in the community. So hope was not completely lost, in spite of the fact that he was tied up in ropes when the girl was being led off to the place of sacrifice. As the camera switched back and forth between the hero in his bonds and the heroine, being dragged towards a bed of coals, the helpers struggled with the hundreds of knots and Sandra—not daring to swallow the last drops of water in case she missed something—whispered, "Hurry, hurry up."

The ending used the same back-and-forth device: although the captain was now freed, he had to get to the girl in time. He raced across the island, while she—surrounded by a muttering mob of fanatic acolytes—gained a few minutes of life; the high priest had to chant the right words over her before she could be thrown into the fiery pit. Close by her stretched a long, burning track of live coals. That was the testing place for liars. You were supposed to have an even chance of getting to the other side if you were telling the truth. But three people had already burst into flames halfway to the finishline and Sandra knew, from the way things were shown, that they'd been telling the truth. Of course, that kind of thing wouldn't work. It was like those penalties for witches: if they sank, they were innocent; if they floated, they were in league with the devil. But at least on the coals you'd have the possibility of escape. If you were in the pit, you stayed there until you burned to a crisp.

The hero ran, the heroine wriggled and screamed, the high priest intoned gloatingly. Behind and above him the perfect diamond sparkled with light. It seemed like an object from another world. The mob—louder and more restive by the minute—kept looking up at it. The priest droned, the heroine moaned, the hero raced. And at last, just as the captain broke on to the scene, another element was added: a sudden, deep rumbling. Way off in the background, smoke began to rise from the volcano. The sky darkened, the grumbling was like thunder, the earth shook. Everyone screamed, even the two hulking guards who were holding the girl. The hero ran up and took her by the hand. But the high priest, seeing him, pointed and shouted to his priestly warriors. They moved forward, their spears ready. The escape route was cut off. The only way out was to go through the fire.

Sandra leaned over to put her glass down on the floor without taking her eyes from the screen. The volcano erupted, showering sparks and ashes everywhere. Hero and heroine dashed through the mob and reached the fiery walkway, which—miraculously—they negotiated without harm, although parts of their clothing exploded into a bright, gassy cloud around them. They reached the far side and stepped out on to the ground. That was the kind of thing true love enabled you to do. The high priest was in fits. He ordered people to go after them. A few started out, but the fire engulfed them. And suddenly everybody realized that the priest wasn't helping. In fact, he was spending most of his time sending other people to their death. What was left of the mob advanced on him. His bodyguards tried to protect him, but when they saw that the maddened crowd was backing them into a corner with him, they quit worrying about their leader and tried to save themselves.

The phone rang. Sandra knocked over a stack of cassette tapes to get to it fast; she thought it would be Bert, repentant and sentimental, ready to propose something really nice, to make up.

It was her Aunt Marion. They didn't see each other very often. Aunt Marion had always been independent. But in the past three years six of her friends had died and once more

106

her family had become a necessity to her, though she still didn't like them much.

"Is something wrong?" Sandra asked.

"Nothing bad, dear. No, just inconvenient. I'm supposed to be away for the weekend, but now the only day the men can deliver the window is Saturday. They can't even take it to McHutchin's, because he's in Bangor for his son's wedding. And I couldn't cancel my outing with Elsie." Elsie was one of the two surviving friends. "I don't suppose you could let them in for me, could you?"

"I guess I could." So far, Aunt Marion had proved to be someone who appreciated and returned favors, not a person who took acts of kindness to mean encouragement towards further—and possibly, unending—imposition. "What time did they say they'd deliver the thing?"

"In the afternoon. 'Sometime after noon,' they said. You know how they are."

"What time are you leaving?"

"Oh, early. As early as possible. But you could get the key from, um, the usual place, you know."

Sandra knew. One of the reasons why her aunt had singled her out was that she was quick to pick up that sort of hint. There were other members of the family who were more cheerful or obliging, but some of them were pretty dense. "I remember," she said. "I won't repeat it over the phone. Yes, sure. I can be there about ten o'clock."

"How kind of you, Sandra. That really is a relief. If that window doesn't go in soon, I can see myself waiting all winter for it. You're an angel."

"As a matter of fact, it could work out very well. I've got a lot to think about over the next couple of days."

"A boyfriend?" Aunt Marion too was fairly quick on the draw. "I hope it's something nice."

Sandra laughed. She said she wasn't sure: she probably wouldn't know about that until she'd done the thinking.

"I'll make up the bed in the guest room," her aunt said. "The second on the left, at the top of the stairs. And there's plenty of food in the icebox."

"I'll be there," Sandra told her. "And if you leave a phone number, I'll call you."

Aunt Marion said that that would be perfect and Sandra was truly a friend in need. She hung up.

As soon as she put the receiver down, Sandra began to think it was possible that all the time she'd been talking to her aunt, Bert might have tried to get in touch with her. Maybe she should call him up, to find out: to see if he'd changed his mind. He could come with her to Aunt Marion's; spend the weekend. She'd have to ask first.

She lifted the receiver and immediately put it down again. That would be weak and silly. And if she felt angry at herself, it was—naturally—his fault. He was the one she should be mad at.

The adventure movie still rampaged across the television screen. She stepped back into the living room. The mob yelled and brandished spears, while fire shot up into the sky like celebration rockets. She sat back down in her chair.

The hero and heroine made a rush for the cool jungle and the sea beyond, where his boat was waiting. In the background you could see the priest being thrown into the burning pit, his two guards following him. The sound of their screams was covered by the roaring of flames, the crack and crashing of the volcano. Sparks rained from the sky. Hero and heroine speeded up, but things didn't look good. As they entered the tall foliage, the earth was shaken by new rumblings, the idol shuddered on its pedestal. The crowd groaned and the statue split, sending the diamond vaulting high into the air, projected like a shooting star over the heads of the embroiled mob.

It fell right in front of the escaping lovers. The heroine gasped. She bent down to where it lay nested in a halo of light, its outlines almost hidden by the twinkling sparkles of its radiance. Her hand opened towards it. But the hero pulled her back. He kicked the jewel out of the way and dragged her forward. They crashed through the trees. Behind them the vegetation became an incandescent river of writhing flames and whizzing fireballs. They reached the shore, plunged into the water, swam to the boat. And the last anyone saw of them was their embracing forms against the white sail of *The Dauntless.* The boat slipped quickly away from the burning island. Every sail was full, straining towards freedom. And large letters spelled out the words "The End" over the two faces as they approached each other from left and right for a central clinch—the ecstatic kiss that was to be both conclusion and beginning. Sandra sighed. She relaxed. Right up to the end, she'd been worried that something would go wrong.

There were other shows to watch afterwards, but she'd had enough. He wasn't going to call.

She took the bath she'd been putting off. Then she brushed her teeth. If he'd tried to phone, that was too bad.

She sat propped up in bed with a magazine open on her lap. She read for a while, but she lost interest. Her mind kept going back to the South Sea island in the movie: the exotic jungle, the pagan crowds baying for blood, the idol that guarded its shimmering diamond, the escape of the two lovers as the island went up like a torch. That was what she loved about the movies—they gave you everything like a dream. It wasn't just that she liked them, even though they weren't true: she liked them precisely because they weren't. In real life, what would have happened to the hero and heroine? That would have been a different kind of human sacrifice. She could imagine it: eight years later, the two of them trying to make a living in an American city somewhere; the heroine would look back and say to herself, *I had a fortune right in front of me and he kicked it away. What kind of fool would do that? We could have lived like kings.* And he'd be thinking, *If only I'd gone for the diamond and not the girl. I'd be happy now, have new women whenever I liked, and my own boat again—my own island, if I wanted it; freedom for the rest of my days, and a good life for all my children, even if I had hundreds of them.*

And what would have happened to the diamond? It would be all right, even if the island sank to the bottom of the sea. It was not, like human love, vulnerable to change. That was the trick to real life: you could walk through fire for each other and still end up wishing you'd never married.

She put the magazine on the night table and turned out the light.

THE NEXT MORNING she packed a nightgown, the summer sandals she wore as bedroom slippers, the book she'd been intending for months to read straight through. She set out early enough to miss the traffic in town.

It was a cloudy fall day but the sky looked as if the weather might clear up later. It had been a bad year for trees. The long drought in June and July—maybe even the strange spring weather before that—had done something to their leaves: instead of turning color, they'd just dried up and gone brown. Halloween was less than a week away and still there had been no beautiful trees to look at. Everyone felt disappointed. It was like seeing a spring when the fruit trees failed to blossom.

All night long she'd expected the call from Bert. Now she was glad that she knew how things were. She was also happy to get away from the city for a few days. She drove fast. Before she arrived, the sun came out. She hummed a little tune as she entered the neat, picturebook suburb in which Aunt Marion had a medium-sized frame house surrounded by flowerbeds, lawn, picket fence and everything else her neighbors had too. It seemed a nice place to live—peaceful and pretty, and not—as she used to think of such districts—dull, houseproud and undoubtedly full of bigots.

Aunt Marion had left a note by the telephone. There were instructions about the stove, the lights, how to double-lock the front door and what to do to the handle of the guest-room toilet if the water kept running. A long list of foods followed—all the delicacies Sandra could and should help herself to. And then there was the information about the window. Sandra had trouble reading the name of the delivery firm, but she got as far as Lo-something. She put the note into her pocket and went to the kitchen. She inspected the icebox crammed with food. It almost looked as though her aunt had spent the night cooking meals for her: a fish casserole, puddings, cold chicken and ham. There were glass containers of peas and rice. And in the cold room were two cakes, several full jars of cookies, fudge and walnut brownies. Unless Aunt

Marion had made a lot of new friends recently, she must have been holding bridge parties at her house, or entertaining people from the garden club she belonged to.

Sandra walked back to the dining room and on to the living room. It had been several months since she'd been in the house, yet everything seemed to be exactly as when she'd last seen it. She took her suitcase upstairs. Most of her visits to Aunt Marion had been for the day. She hadn't spent the night in one of the guest rooms since her childhood. And it had been years since she'd stayed long enough to explore the neighborhood.

She unpacked. After that, she wandered downstairs again. The house was beginning to feel strange. It was an odd thing about empty houses; this one felt quiet in a way that wasn't restful. It was as if the absence of the owner had brought on a parallel absence within the house: as if the air had died.

She got out her book. As she read, the sun outside brightened and warmed the room around the big, high-backed chair she'd chosen. She sank deep into the story. It was about a southern belle who was falling in love with a scoundrel; he wanted to take over her family's plantation. The heroine was struggling hard against her feelings and wondering whether she ought to let him dance with her at the cotillion, when the doorbell rang. Sandra jumped.

She opened the door without bothering to look first. It could have been anyone, but in a suburb like this it would be ridiculous to suspect the kind of attack that happened in big cities. Life wasn't like that here.

Three hefty workmen stood on her aunt's gray-and-white painted porch. One of them—the one in charge—had rung the bell. The two others held between them a large pane of glass in a frame; they had rested it where it was just about to dig into one of the strategically placed potted geraniums that made the porch look so cheerful and welcoming, or—as Sandra had once believed—so maddeningly tidy. All three men wore white overalls. The leader had removed his cap.

She welcomed them with a smile, showed them through the house and opened a door next to the pantry, where Aunt Marion had said the window should go. Gardening equipment and vases had been pushed back to make room. When the time came to slide the window into its space, the man in authority lent a hand. "Over to the right," he told the others. "Don't let her down yet. Look out for the edge there, Jake." It all went smoothly. Nothing was broken or knocked over. Everyone seemed pleased. Sandra thanked the men profusely. She told them how delighted her aunt would be. They said they were glad to help out: you needed the windows to be right, now that the cold was coming on. The one named Jake gave her a little wave and all three trooped out.

She closed the door behind them. She hadn't offered a tip, since Aunt Marion's note had expressly cautioned her not to let the men have anything. *I've given them plenty already,* she had written, *and this window is late.*

She waited until the workmen had driven away, then her city habits forced her back to the front door. She put the chain on and turned the lock.

All the rest of the morning she read. She made herself a sandwich and salad lunch, listened to some music on the radio and went out for a walk. She could have driven to another town, gone to a museum or tried to get into an afternoon show somewhere, but she felt that she was responsible for keeping an eye on the house. She didn't think that she should get too far away. If the year and the trees had been better, she'd have cruised around the countryside and looked at the fall colors.

While she walked, she thought about Bert, about how she was going to start regular exercise at the Y this year—swimming or aerobics; about whether she could afford to go away in the spring and, if so, where she should go. She realized all at once that if she could get together the money for a really nice trip somewhere, she wouldn't want to take it with Bert. If he were with her, her time would be spent in paying attention to him, not absorbing new sights and thoughts. Maybe he'd felt the same way. That could be the reason why he hadn't wanted to spend the weekend with her.

She'd been out walking around the neighborhood with her aunt twice before: once when she was about eight years old, and once again three years before her Great-Aunt Constance had died. On that visit they'd gone to look at a nearby memorial—a bronze statue erected to a woman who had dressed as a soldier in order to follow her husband into battle during the time of the Revolution. Sandra remembered the statue as pretty and looking rather like the portrait of a musician, although—perhaps because of the ponytail hairstyle—too obviously a woman.

She walked until she realized that as far as the statue went, she was lost. It wasn't to be found in the direction she'd taken. She turned back, trying not to feel upset. Just lately—no doubt because of Bert—whenever anything didn't pan out, she'd add it to her list of what wasn't going right for her.

She would have liked to see the memorial for reasons other than its prettiness. She'd have liked to see the visible corroboration of the woman's story. Of course, it was a famous theme: the loyal wife. And she remembered that there was a folksong, supposedly based on fact, about another woman from farther south, who had also tried to join her husband at the war but hadn't been able to get across the river at one stage; she'd had to follow the river for miles, all the way up north. It had taken her about three years, until nearly the end of the fighting.

She couldn't remember if the woman had found her husband in the end. Probably, for the song to make sense, she must have, although in a way that didn't matter. It was the effort that counted. Some women were just brave: they would try. Where did they find the reserves of courage—was it simply necessity that brought out noble action in people? That couldn't be all there was to it. You had to be pretty good to begin with. The woman in the folksong had had children: sometimes motherhood made timid women strong. But often it worked the other way—it wore them down. And was it a sign of strength to leave your children in times of trouble, or was it better to stay with them? There really were no rules for behavior. Half the time she didn't even understand her own actions. But she knew that nothing would have persuaded her to pick up a gun and go off to the wars dressed like the young Mozart. She'd have crawled into a hole somewhere and waited till the action was over. Perhaps it was an appreciation of her cowardice that made her admire these decisive, revolutionary women; she wasn't particularly impressed by men who were of the same, heroic type. Men were supposed to be like that. Men of action were nothing special. They liked it. It was a biological compulsion, or so she'd been led to believe.

It was still light when she got back to the house. She had

time to make herself a cup of tea, sit down again with her book and get through the villain's seduction of the heroine's cousin, before she had to turn on a lamp.

She was somewhere among the arguments about what the Dred Scott Decision had done to influence ordinary people's lives, when the doorbell rang again. She switched on more lights, including the one outside on the porch. It was quite likely that the delivery men had just discovered that they'd brought her the wrong thing earlier in the day.

This time she looked, leaning to the side and peering at the gauze-covered panel windows to the left and right of the door. She saw no delivery men. She saw a child: a small boy of about ten, who was dressed in a jacket and tie, as if he were going to a party. She assumed that he was one of the children whose parents had decided to set Halloween on the weekend, rather than on Monday.

She undid the chain, opened the door and said hello.

"Um, good evening," he said. He stood there smiling and nervous, and as if he couldn't think of anything else to say.

"I'm afraid I wasn't expecting any Halloween callers to-night," she told him. "And besides, why aren't you wearing a costume?"

"Halloween's Monday," he said. "It's not about that. Ah. I need help."

"Are you lost?" Few children got lost after the age of six or seven, but it was an explanation she was always ready to accept. She got lost all the time herself.

"Yes," he said. "That's right. I'm lost."

"Well, you'd better come in, I guess." She held the door open. He walked in after her. She led the way to the living room and to the hallway where the telephone sat on its table. "We can call your parents," she said.

"Oh, no, that's just the trouble. I can't." He sat down in a chair quickly, as if he'd be safer there. He held on tight to his knees. His look of discomfort seemed to be based on something other than the fact that he was too small for the chair. "It's a long story," he said. "And it sounds weird."

She sat down in the chair facing his. "Well, you just tell me," she said. She'd never been the mainstay and comfort of a child before. She felt like a fake. She'd always imagined that motherly talents came naturally after childbirth and probably had something to do with hormones.

"It sounds impossible," he began. "But I didn't want to go to the police."

"Why not?"

"Well, you know what the cops are like. They've got their hands full already. They won't want to take care of some kid who's off his rocker. They'd put me in a psychiatric ward." As he began to talk, he stopped looking so jittery. And his gestures, his facial expressions, were like those of an adult: matter-of-fact and easy.

"Would they?" she said.

"Sure."

"What's your name?"

"Roy," he said. He added absently, "It means king."

"I'm Sandra."

Roy held out his hand, shook her hand, said, "How do you do?" and sat back in his chair again, like a businessman who was ready to begin a discussion. "Do you believe in magic?" he asked.

"Taking rabbits out of hats? Making things disappear?"

"No, no. Not the stuff you can see in a show. Like the fairytales. Making things change. Turning somebody into a stone. Or into—something else, maybe."

"A prince turning into a frog, you mean? Or the other way around?"

"That's right. You think it's possible?"

"Does this have something to do with Halloween?"

"No. At least, I don't think so. But I hadn't thought of that. I guess we're coming up to that time of the year, aren't we? Is it the equinox or the solstice? I always forget."

"The equinox. Daylight Saving is tomorrow. And Halloween is on Monday. Like you said."

"Um. You'd think if that had anything to do with it, it would have happened right on the day. Not one or two days before."

"Just tell me, Roy. What's happened?"

"Okay. I'll tell it to you like a story. There's this eleven-year-old kid. His father got divorced over a year and a half ago."

"Yes."

"And she married somebody else. Some guy with two kids of his own. And they didn't like this boy. So, he kept saying to his father that it was no good—he wanted to live with him."

"Yes," Sandra said. She'd lost track of how many people were in the cast of characters and which "he" was at the center of the action.

"So this boy," he went on, "got to live with his father. And he wouldn't let him alone for a minute, so the father never got to go out with any women: he was going crazy. Then this kid saw some kind of show on TV—I don't know what it was; and he got all interested in magic. He asked for a couple of books, and he'd sit in his room doing things like—oh, incantations, I guess. And then this morning I woke up, and look at me."

"Yes?"

"How old do you think I am?"

She didn't want to offend him by guessing too young. He might be small for his age. "I'm not very good at judging how old people are," she said.

"I look about eleven, don't I?"

"About that."

"I'm thirty-four. It's my son who's eleven."

He waited for her to take in what he'd said. She stared at him. He shrugged finally, and looked down at the floor. When she still didn't say anything, he muttered, "I told you, it sounds weird."

She pushed herself forward in her chair. "Would you like a cup of tea?" she asked. "I was just about to make another one when you rang the bell."

"What I'd really like is a good, stiff drink, but I don't know if I could take it. Maybe a Coke, or something."

"How about a Sprite?" She couldn't remember if there were any Coca-Colas in the icebox.

"Fine. I'm not out of my mind, you know."

"You don't seem to be. But I've got to get used to the idea. Let me think a little. I'll get things ready." She got up and walked into the kitchen.

First, she put the kettle on. Then, she opened the icebox and took out a bottle of Sprite. It wasn't until she started to look for the icecubes that she began to feel incensed. It was a joke, of course: a kind of pre-Halloween prank, or possibly the date was coincidental and he was just trying this out for fun, to see how people would take it. There were really only two questions to consider: did he know what he was doing, or was he lost in some other way, so that he was driven to throw himself on the mercy of strangers? After all, he was only a child, even though he appeared to be extremely self-possessed.

She thought he must know what he was doing. That might not mean that he was wholly malicious. It would probably be the usual thing: unhappy at home. If that were the answer, his father would seem to be the main culprit; no matter what background story the boy had told, the central theme was concerned with his father.

She took the glass into the living room and handed it to him. "There you go," she said. Behind her in the kitchen the kettle started to whistle. She ran back.

There was also the problem of whether this game of fooling the neighbors was a first attempt or a regular practice. If it were the first time, her reactions could be crucial to his future emotional state. That might also hold true if this were a habit. He was definitely a very smart little boy. He'd managed to make up a story that would prevent her from wanting to return him to a parent and that, at the same time, would make her think twice about getting in touch with the police.

Well, she thought, *poor thing*. Her own upbringing had been distinctly old-fashioned, boringly solid: no divorce, no embattled couples or extramarital allegiances. She hadn't liked her childhood, but she'd always known where she stood. Children nowadays sometimes couldn't figure out what they were supposed to be. They ended up being given more advice and information by television programs than by their parents. Come to think of it, she'd once seen a movie on TV about this very subject: a comedy about a father and son who changed places. The transformation had had something to do with an object that had occult powers, like the magic lamp in *Aladdin*; one of the characters, either father or son, had made a wish. And the wish had switched them both around. This little boy, Roy, had probably seen some similar comedy episode. He'd simply altered it to suit his needs; that was what grown people did all the time, only they learned to tone down their fictions. The sheer outrageousness of his story was a sign of innocence.

She carried the teacup carefully. As she approached her chair, she said, "I shouldn't have filled this so full." She was always doing that and because she couldn't drink anything too hot she'd have to leave it full and then she'd spill some. This time her hand was steady. She got the saucer on to the table and sat down. "So," she said, "what am I going to do with you?"

"You don't believe me."

"I guess I can't understand how you could change a person from one body into another. I mean, just to begin with: the mind is part of the body. They grow together. So, if you had a different body, you'd be a different person. See what I mean?"

"I don't understand it, either. But it happened."

"What I do believe is that you're in some kind of trouble."

"I haven't done anything. If you call the police, I'll run away again. They'd take me back to him. And I don't know what he'd do. He might even kill me. He could do it. He's bigger than I am now. And stronger. All that time I spent at the gym—Jesus."

"Am I the first person you came to for help?"

"I tried two others. The first one lived right down the road. She actually called my son. My father. You know. I realize it sounds crazy. What am I supposed to do?"

"That's the problem. And what am I supposed to do? That's another one. I can't keep you here. Nobody can just let you stay. And if you're stuck that way, what are you going to do about your job?"

"Oh, he'll do that. He's going to be better at it than I was."

"Really? What's your line of work?"

"I do the advertising for a big firm of toy manufacturers."

"Isn't that very specialized? You deal with accounts and presentation and all that?"

He waved his hand. "He's a natural," he said.

She almost burst out laughing. To pretend to be his father, who was describing him in praiseworthy terms, must be making him feel good in several ways at once. *It's like the theater,* she thought. *And I'm the audience.* "What about your mother?" she asked. "That is: your ex-wife; wouldn't she understand?"

"Her? Are you kidding?"

"You don't think it's worth a try?"

"She didn't even understand when everything was normal."

"Well, sometimes that's the way it is. You don't see other people's worries until they're brought to your attention."

"She wouldn't be interested. She wants her own life."

"You're still part of her life, aren't you? You're part of a family."

"No, listen. She wouldn't believe me. She'd think I was doing it to get a rise out of her. Let's stop talking about her."

"All right. What about your son?"

"What about him?"

"The way this thing works, he looks like you now and you look like him—is that right?"

"That's right. He's got my body. And my face and voice and the car keys and the bank balance and the woman I've been going out with for the past couple of weeks; except, I don't think he knows about that yet. But I guess he'll find out."

"He can't use the car, though."

"Oh, he can drive. I taught him last summer."

"Well."

"Uh-huh."

"When did all this happen?"

"Thursday."

"When was the exact moment?"

"I was trying to get him to go to bed and he wouldn't. He used every trick he knew, distracting and delaying. But eventually he got into bed and I turned out the light and went downstairs. I was a little drunk. You know, you finally get out and have a nice meal with somebody and come back, pay the babysitter, and you think that's the end. And then he starts up again. I could hear him working on his computer. He does that a lot. By the time I get up the stairs, he's back in bed again, pretending to be asleep. Then, he lies. He says the machine works on its own sometimes."

"Do you think that could be true?"

"What?"

"That the machine has something to do with whatever happened?"

"Oh, no. It's him."

"And the babysitter?"

"Karen. She's fine. She's a girl from our neighborhood. Not like that other one he found for last night: Debbie. The minute he was out of the door, she started pulling all my clothes off—I couldn't believe it. She carried me to the bathroom—she carried me. She was huge. I couldn't do anything. I was kicking and yelling and everything. It was like she was deaf. I mean, she was like a robot. She threw me into the bathtub and started to scrub me raw. It was awful. I was humiliated. I guess she thought that was what babysitters were supposed to do. Unless she was crazy. She didn't make me brush my teeth. I actually had to ask to do that. Jees. I bet he did it on purpose."

Sandra stood up and snapped on the ceiling light and two of the lower lamps. The more he talked, the more she thought that she really shouldn't have invited him in. Now that he was there, she had to listen. And then what? She couldn't send him away in the dark. And she didn't like the idea of turning him in to the police. To hand a child over to the state's official body of law enforcement would be a gross act of betrayal. Children weren't criminals just because they ran away.

There had been a story in the news once, a few years ago, about a boy who had run away from his parents; he'd managed all on his own to get to his grandmother's house, some two hundred and fifty miles away. And when he'd arrived, his grandmother had immediately phoned the police. Whenever Sandra thought about that story, she was filled with outrage. Everyone she knew had agreed with her at the time: it was a horrible thing to do. How could a child trust anyone after that?

She said, "Do you think maybe something he did with the computer was what started it all?"

"I don't understand how it could have. But I don't see how any of this could happen from any other cause, either."

"You heard the computer from downstairs."

"That's right. And I ran up again to shut it off. I was ready to wipe the whole thing. He's got games and all kinds of things in storage. He knows a lot more than I do. He was always winning prizes at those children's clubs he belonged to. And then later, he'd win all the games you can plug into."

"Would you say he's smarter than you are?"

"Oh, he thinks so."

"You don't?"

"I think he's crazy. He's sick. You can't call somebody intelligent if he's not . . . well, listen: a couple of years ago he had a pet hamster. He called it Schizo. It died. I don't think he was feeding it the right stuff. Or maybe he was doing nutritional experiments on it—that's what he said he did to the goldfish. Anyway, after it died, he wanted us to call him Schizo, instead of Eric. We found out he'd gotten all his friends at school to do it. One day Ginette answered the phone and there was this kid on the other end of the line, saying, 'I'd like to speak to Schizo, please.' Now, that's too much, isn't it? That's over the edge."

"If you're unhappy, nothing's beyond the limit. He was trying to keep the memory of his pet alive, wasn't he? And I guess he's unhappy about the divorce, too."

"Oh, the divorce puts him in a perfect position. He can have power over all of us. The hamster business was something else. That had to do with a thing called atavars, or avatars, I forget which. I wouldn't be surprised if he'd killed it as part of a ritual. He doesn't feel affection, you know. He likes to have the upper hand."

He likes to rule, Sandra thought. *Roy means king.* She couldn't figure out whether the story he was telling about his family was the way he'd meant to outline it, or whether her sympathetic reaction had caused him to change some masterplan he'd tried out before. He'd already talked to other people: that was what he said, although that too might be a lie.

"What's his name again?"

"Eric."

"Was that the only time he asked you to call him by a different name?"

"What scares me," he said, "is that he's getting better at it. The first time, it only lasted a few minutes."

"What?"

"The switch-around. And the second time was for three hours. I just hid in the room till it was over."

"It happened before? This is—"

"The third time."

"Okay. I see. There's probably a pattern that'll help to show how it operates."

"I don't think so. The first two times, it happened while I was asleep. I woke up different. Changed. First time, in the morning. And the second time was in the afternoon—I'd just dropped off, having a nap. This time, I ran up the stairs, opened his door and got the lightswitch, and that did it. The light—it was as if the light caused it. I thought I'd been electrocuted. But there I was, all of a sudden: him. And he was sitting up in bed, saying, 'Hi, Schizo.' "

"What clothes did you have on?"

"Why?"

"When you turned on the light, you changed size. What happened to the clothes?"

"Oh, yes. That was funny. I had on this huge suit."

"And the shoes?"

"Same thing. I had to step out of them."

"What about Eric? He was sitting up in bed and he'd just been changed, too. So, he was full-sized. Whose pajamas was he wearing?"

"He doesn't. He won't wear pajamas."

His answer wasn't quite quick enough. These things always broke down on the detail, like theories of life after death.

Something was going on. There was no way she could know exactly what, but that didn't matter. She'd caught the gist of it: that this undersized child felt an overwhelming need to take over the position of father, so that he would no longer be helpless. To pretend that his father had become a child would be paying him back for all sorts of things, including the divorce. But he hadn't worked out the finer points of his story.

He'd made a mistake in talking too much. He'd over-explained. He should just have told her that his parents were mean to him. If he'd left it simple like that, she might never have moved away from her initial feeling of pity. But she was being asked for too much. It seemed to her now that he was quite strange and rather creepy. She'd give him something to eat and then call up a rescue squad. She ought to have done that straight away. She sensed herself edging towards betrayal, telling herself that she wasn't qualified to deal with a child who was obviously so disturbed: that this was a job for professionals. She'd telephone somebody. She'd have to. While they'd been talking, while the light had grown less and had at last disappeared, he'd become her responsibility.

"Are you hungry?" she asked. "I think I'll fix myself something to eat. Come on into the kitchen." She got up and walked ahead of him.

AS SOON as he saw what was in the icebox, he went to work. Without asking her what she wanted to save or how much he was being offered, he pulled out dishes, bowls and jars. He dropped bread into the toaster and asked where the plates were. He'd just put the finishing touches on a toasted club sandwich when the telephone rang. He froze, his hand covering the food as if he'd stolen it.

"It's probably my aunt," she told him. She walked into the hall and picked up the receiver.

"Sandra?" Aunt Marion said. "Did Lomax & Kidder send the men?"

"Oh yes, that's fine. I mean, it seems to be. I haven't measured it, but I'm sure it's okay. It looks the right size."

Aunt Marion was pleased. She asked in a general way if Sandra was all right; if she needed anything. All the arrangements were just fine, Sandra said: they'd see each other soon. She hung up. She'd forgotten to ask about directions for finding the statue of the revolutionary heroine. She'd been thinking all the time about the boy in the kitchen.

He was halfway through his sandwich when she got back. She put two more slices of bread into the toaster.

"Was that your boyfriend?" he said.

"That was my aunt. My great-aunt. She wanted to know about the storm window."

"Why?"

She wasn't going to explain everything to him, to tell him that it wasn't her house and that she was a guest almost as much as he was. She snatched the hot toast out of the machine and threw it on to her plate. "Why not?" she asked.

"Just asking. You aren't married, are you?"

"No."

"Is your boyfriend coming back tonight?"

"Maybe. Why?"

"Well, if he's away or something, maybe I could stay over."

"No."

"Just for tonight. It would make a big difference. It would mean he couldn't find me."

"I can't let you stay here. That's definite."

"You don't know what he's like."

"Don't you have any ideas about what I can do with you? I don't want to hand you over to the police, but what else can I do?"

"You can keep me right here."

"Would you rather go to a kind of shelter place, or to a hospital, or to the social workers?"

"I don't want to go to any of those places. They'd just send me back to him."

"I don't think so. Not if you really made a fuss."

"They wouldn't believe me."

"Well, don't tell them everything. Just tell them that he treats you badly and you're scared of him and you don't want to go back."

"They wouldn't care. They'd all start persuading. People talk and talk at you, till you lose hope. And then you just agree to what they decide."

"Some of those places give you a lawyer."

She sat down at the kitchen table to eat her sandwich. She'd cut it into four sections. As she picked one of them up, he asked, "Can I have some of your sandwich?"

She pushed the plate towards him.

They ate in silence for a while, then he said, "If Jesus Christ came back now, what do you think would happen to him?"

She chewed. Did he think of himself as a misunderstood Messiah—was he aiming that high? "He'd be a rock star," she said. "He'd capture the audience and then he'd get born again and try to take everybody with him."

"I don't think so. I think he'd be betrayed again. I know it always happens, sooner or later. They just can't believe you."

She waited. He bit into his quarter of the sandwich. At any minute he might claim to be The Second Coming. Or maybe he'd go for broke and announce that he was an alien.

HE MIGHT just want some sympathy. Or he might be out of his mind. The mentally ill came in all shapes and all ages. So did con artists. And you could see anything on television nowadays: you could be excited by the idea of trying out something you'd seen. This might be a practice run, like a rehearsal. It would take a lot of nerve, of course. There couldn't be many children who would engage strange grown-ups in conversation—that was a thing they were always being warned against. Even if they weren't scared, they'd expect an unfavorable response. But a lonely boy, without brothers and sisters at home or friends at school, might be driven to make contact with other people: this meeting with a stranger might be a way of asking for advice. It could also, just as easily, be a joke he'd cooked up with his friends. If a joke, how harmless was it? And who else was in on it? She was all alone in the house. Maybe she'd better think about that.

She also began to wonder to what extent their acquaintance was a matter of chance. Had he picked her out at random, or had he chosen her specially? It was possible that he'd seen her out walking earlier in the day, and had followed her to see where she lived. That wasn't a nice thought. The picture of a lost and sad little boy didn't agree with such predatory action.

He said, "If Jesus Christ was alive today, they'd say he was loony."

"They'd probably just say he was a Communist, unless he started boasting about who his father was. He'd have to keep a low profile."

"What does that mean?"

"Keep his head down, so nobody could see him against the skyline. But you're assuming that all those miracles and things are true."

"If Jesus Christ was alive today," he said again, "his own mother would turn him over to the cops."

Not his mother, Sandra thought, *nor his wife. They don't. You can read in the newspapers about maniacs and murderers or rapists, and almost always they have families; they're married. The wives and mothers have to know some of what's going on. Part of them doesn't know, part of them does. But they never say anything. The unspoken, unacknowledged evil in families, society, in politics, isn't condemned because—if once recognized—something would have to be done about it. And then our world would come to an end. Our world is the one where we don't do it ourselves, but we can see the advantages to be gained by keeping quiet about it.*

"His mother wouldn't," she said, "but the neighbors might."

She was beginning to feel as if that kind of traditional neighborly interference might make sense. No matter what they were like or what might have happened between them, his father and mother would be worried to death. She had only his word for it that they were even divorced. She ought to turn him in to somebody who could deal with him.

But not against his will. At the moment he seemed relaxed. It was insidiously agreeable to imagine that he considered her a sympathetic listener and therefore, by inference, a better parent than either of his real ones. There was no denying that he was odd but something about him, from the beginning, had appealed to her. Why had he chosen her to unburden himself to—to put on this performance? Why did people choose each other?

"How did all this begin?" she asked.

"I told you. With the computer."

"I mean: when did you notice that things were going wrong between you?" *I sound like the advertisements in a True Romance magazine,* she thought: *When was it that you first spotted those telltale signs that his love was waning?*

"It all goes back to six years ago," he said. "At Christmas."

"Was that when the marriage split up?"

"No, that was less than two years ago. It wasn't anything to do with that. This was just him. It began with his Christmas present. He'd asked for a magic wand. Nothing else. He said afterwards that he figured he wouldn't have to ask for anything else, because once he had the wand, he could get whatever he made a wish for. That was a disaster. He was so disappointed, he cried. He kept saying, 'It doesn't work.' And he blamed it on us. He couldn't see why we'd lie to him like that."

"Didn't you warn him? That it wouldn't really be magic?"

"Of course not. That's silly. Everybody knows that."

"I can remember seeing one of those tricks at the circus. I thought it really was magic, but I was pretty sure it wasn't the wand that caused it. Or the cloak and hat, or anything like that. I thought it was the person. I thought he was using something like electricity."

"He thought it was the wand." He wasn't interested in her childhood memories. "You think I could have another sandwich?" he said.

"Sure."

She sat with her elbow bent and her chin in her hand, while he made himself another large sandwich. He'd dropped his guard. All his physical actions seemed comfortable. He was no longer pretending to be a man who had suddenly found himself half the size he was used to being. He must have come to the conclusion that he could count on her allegiance; whereas she, on the contrary, had suddenly had enough. He was too peculiar. Although his story, and the way he was presenting it to her, had its touching and amusing aspects, to hear someone talking about himself in the third person was beginning to annoy her. She remembered with amazement that he, a child, had managed to put her in a position where she was eager to believe that an utterly impossible, supernatural event had taken place. She was right—it wasn't the wand, it was the electricity.

As he unloaded plates and jars from the icebox, he started up again. "You know how it is," he said, "when you want something really bad. You think about it so hard, for so long. You think: nothing could ever make you want it less. But then you get nervous about losing it before you get to it. And then people—they don't actually try to talk you out of it, but they tell you to turn your attention to something else while you're waiting. So you do. And then somehow, you just forget it. You forget how much it meant. The importance is gone."

"Yes," she said. That was desire: there was a time-limit attached to it. To be grown up wasn't so marvelous, once you were there. It could only seem wonderful to a child. She hadn't understood that when she was younger. But he did. He already knew about desire.

"This might be building up," he said. "That could happen to me. I could just forget my life."

"I don't think so."

"It's possible. It happens to people."

"Amnesia?"

"I meant: forget that I'm me, so that everybody thinks he's me. But I guess I could get amnesia, too."

"I got interested in amnesia once. It's sort of scary to think about. But it usually only happens after a shock or if you get hit on the head, like concussion or something. Sometimes a big mental shock will start it, but then it only happens to a certain kind of person."

"What kind?"

"The kind that can't face things."

"I didn't put enough mayonnaise in this one," he told her. "It's good but it needs just a little—"

"I'll get it," she said. She stood up, took a few steps over to the icebox and had her fingers on the doorhandle when the front doorbell rang.

He jumped up. She got the mayonnaise out and handed it to him. He held on to it as if it were some kind of protection. "Don't let anybody in," he said.

"It's all right. I'll just go see who it is. You finish your sandwich."

SHE WALKED back through the dining room, the hall, and past the living room. A young man stood outside the front door. He looked like an executive type, not the sort of person to be selling anything door to door or to know her Aunt Marion. A step up from Bert, anyway. Perhaps something had gone wrong with his car or his telephone. Or maybe he was another one who was lost. The knowledge that one other person was in the house—even though underage and possibly not right in the head—made her feel safe against intruders. She opened the door.

He smiled. He said that he was sorry to disturb her.

"That's all right."

"I wonder if you've seen a boy, about eleven: my son." He raised a hand as if to indicate a flood level, and added, "About this high. Hair kind of, um, more or less like mine. Eyes . . ."

He was better-looking than his son, though it was impossible to tell how eleven-year-olds were going to turn out, especially in the matter of looks. He seemed completely all right and normal, not a cruel father or a man who was claiming to be something he wasn't.

"I did see a boy when I was out walking this afternoon," she said. "He was coming from the direction of town, over there, and I passed him on my way back here. Has something happened?"

"What did he look like?"

"He was on the other side of the street. He just looked like a schoolboy. You know. Except that he was all dressed up."

"That's right. He was supposed to be going to a party, but he didn't. He skipped out of it."

"Is he in some kind of trouble?"

"No, no. This happens periodically. He runs off for a while. Anything he doesn't want to do."

"It might have been some other boy. I don't know. If I see him again, should I phone the police?"

"No, don't do that. Here. I'll give you my phone number." He took a notebook and a pen out of his breast pocket. From inside the book he produced a business card, which he handed to her. "And I wonder if you'd mind giving me your name. I'm Roy Martinson: it's on the card. My son's called Eric. And this is number—?" He stepped back. His eyes went to the doorframe and the brass numbers on it. "Twenty-three."

"Sandra," she said.

"And do you have a phone number?"

If the house or the telephone had been hers, she would have hesitated. The thought didn't occur to her that by giving out the phone number she might be subjecting her Aunt Marion to a spate of unpleasant anonymous calls. She told him the number.

136

"I've been running around for hours," he said. "and you're the first person I've met who might have seen him beyond Hillside Avenue. Plenty of people saw him at the Perrys', when he was walking out of the party, but they know him in that neighborhood. So, I think I'm going to knock off for a while. Go back home. He might be there already, waiting for me."

"I hope so," she said. Everyone did that: told lies and hypocrisies because they wanted to change things, but couldn't. They wanted to appear helpful and comforting, even when their actions were obstructive. They needed to be liked. She hoped that everything would be all right for him. She wanted him to be happy. But she didn't tell him that his son was in the kitchen.

He thanked her and turned away. She closed the door. She went back to the kitchen, where Eric was sitting behind a pile of jars and plates, his face rigid, his eyes large.

"Well," she said. "I said that I'd seen a boy, just some boy not specified, going in the opposite direction. But I think maybe I ought to call up and get you back home."

"You're a real fool, aren't you?" he said. His tone was so assured, adult and nasty that it stopped her in her tracks. He had a look to go with it. Where did an expression like that come from—from the attractive father?

"Why's that?" she said.

"I know a lot about this house now."

"And I know your father's phone number."

"And I know yours. I think I'll stay. Got some videos we can watch?"

"No."

"Try and make me go."

"That's easy. I pick up the phone and say you arrived just after your father asked about you."

"He isn't my father," the boy screamed. He raised the knife he was holding, until it pointed towards her at a definitely deliberate, offensive angle. Luckily it was one of the kitchen table knives, not a carving knife, but the sharper ones weren't far away. "You'd better not," he shouted at her.

For some reason she wasn't afraid. She didn't believe he could hurt her with a blunt knife. And she was bigger than he was. She stepped up and took the knife away from him. "Don't be silly," she said.

The situation was too much for her. He was too much. Suddenly she just didn't want him in the house. "He seemed," she said, "like a nice man."

"Oh, yeah. Women like him."

They liked him because he made a good impression, even if you didn't count the looks, which made a big difference to begin with. The son made a bad impression, although he'd figured out how to overcome other people's reluctance; he'd kept her talking for hours, persuaded her to invite him to a meal, made her feel guilty about him.

"I like him too," she said. "But if you really don't want to go back to him, I won't call him up. I'll phone the police instead."

"No."

"Then, your mother."

"No, no."

"You choose," she told him. "It's up to you." Three impossible choices—that was freedom. Her own childhood had been like that. She'd never understood why children had to be subjected to that kind of cheating. Now she knew—it was simple; because otherwise, you couldn't get them to do what you wanted them to.

She took out the calling card and went to the phone. She dialed the number.

He didn't move. The phone rang and rang.

She thought that she might have to hang up: the father hadn't had time to get home yet, or he'd gone out again.

There was a click. A man's voice said, "Hello." The voice was a little different, but Sandra recognized it. "Hello," she said. "It's Sandra Beale from Number 23, Wheaten Road. You were asking about your son."

"Is he there?"

"Yes, but he doesn't want—"

"I'll be right over," he said, and hung up. She put the receiver down.

From the kitchen doorway Eric said, "That's not fair. I told you not to."

"That's what you told me," she said, "but sometimes people say things they don't really mean, because it's a way of playing for time. You know that you've got to settle things with him. He's the one you live with. If you really don't want to stay with him, there's your mother."

"I don't want to live with anybody. I want to live all alone. Like you."

"Well, that's no problem. You'll just have to wait. Till you're grown up. Then you can do it. Do what you like."

"It's too far away," he said miserably.

His father, the real Roy, was at the house in a few minutes. His face was serious. The boy couldn't look at him.

"Come on," he said.

Eric shuffled forward. Roy put an arm around him. "That's

right," he said. He moved a step back and opened the door. Over Eric's head he said, "Thank you," to her, and left. She nodded. She'd done the right thing, but she'd betrayed someone in order to do it; someone who was weaker than she was.

She closed the door after them. She stood there a long while before locking up and putting the chain on.

SHE WENT back to the kitchen and sat down at the table. The evidence of Eric's hunger was everywhere in front of her: jars, open boxes, bottles. She stood up again to put the mayonnaise into the icebox. She was beginning to feel bad.

She cleared up the table, put things back where they were supposed to be, washed the dishes and got out the dustpan and brush. She felt a little better. What was either of them to do with her? They were strangers.

She took a long time cleaning up in the kitchen. To keep herself company, and to stop herself thinking about Eric and Roy, she turned on the radio. She worked until everything was spotless but she was almost ready to start the job all over again. It wasn't so much that her aunt's high standards of housekeeping urged her towards imitation; rather, that she was in the sort of mood that was drawing her deeper into itself.

She cleaned the sink, the counters and tabletop, the floor. Then she made sure that the back door was locked, looked at the windows to see that the catches were on, and turned out some of the lights. She hadn't thought about Bert for hours. It was time to give serious attention to the subject. She'd planned to use some of her time over the weekend doing just that. *Right,* she thought: *Bert. What am I going to do about it?*

Nothing came to her. She didn't have anything in common with him, he took her for granted, she'd never believed that he loved her; and as a matter of fact, she didn't like him enough, either. The hell with him.

She made herself a cup of coffee and took it around the corner into the alcove between the hall and the dining room, where the television set was. Aunt Marion maintained that she looked at the news and nothing else, but Sandra suspected that she watched a couple of quiz shows too, every once in a while. A capacious, stiff-backed armchair was positioned in front of the set. A small table stood to the right of the chair, a footstool in front. In the seat, and against the back, several cushions had been bunched into a second, inner shape. Sandra pulled the chair back a few feet, pushed the pillows around and tried them out in different ways.

She looked at a documentary about an Indian landowner who had made his family property into a nature reserve. Among his many schemes for maintaining the natural balance of plants and animals was one that would restore the original wildlife to the numbers on record before drought, famine, flood and—worst of all—hunters had disrupted the populations. Tigers had died out of the area, but one of the workers in the reserve had brought him a female leopard cub. The film was about how he trained the leopard to go back to the wild.

She watched to the end of the program and then for a little while longer, through the start of a comedy, until she began to yawn. She turned off the machine, checked the doors and windows once again, looked around the kitchen and went upstairs.

She took her book with her. Aunt Marion read a lot, mostly biographies and history books; if she had a few minutes of extra time, she'd pick up her embroidery or her knitting. She was a real person, full of information and practical experience: someone you could take seriously. When she died, she would leave behind many useful things that she'd made herself and given to other people. Her character too was generous. She sometimes dispensed advice, although usually only when asked for it, but all the time—in a transaction as easy as breathing in and out—she gave understanding. Whenever Sandra was with her for a few hours, she could feel herself taking on the way Aunt Marion looked at things. For all her traditionally spinsterish ways, Aunt Marion was a woman whose type was that of a mother. She would know what to do about a runaway child. *Never mind,* Sandra thought. *It's all settled.*

When she was ready for bed, she no longer felt like reading. She left the book on the night table and turned out the light.

She dreamt that she was standing on the outer stairs of a grand plantation mansion. The steps she stood on, the columns at either side, the building behind her, were all white, like the dress she was wearing. She could actually feel the dress, in which she stood as if captured: the skirt went out and down from the waist like the sides of a balloon and she was lashed into the center of its many lacy spheres. As the dream began, she'd been looking outward, evidently expecting someone to arrive, but there wasn't anyone there.

The next thing she knew, she was standing inside the house. She was still waiting, but now she had no view of the outside, nor of the front entrance leading to it. Several men appeared suddenly, carrying something. Of course, she thought: Aunt Marion had told her to let the workmen in. She went forward into another room and met the gang of men. She started to give them directions about where to put the window; she now knew exactly where it was to be. As she pointed to a wall in front of her, there—as if it had been there all along, and not made up by her on the spur of the moment—was the empty space where the window was to fit.

The men went to work. The window was in place. She was alone again. But once more she could see—looking through the newly installed window to the front of the house—the steps, the carriageway and the garden beyond. The window became a door. A man walked up the steps and rang the bell. She could see through: it was Eric's father, Roy. He said, as before, "I hope I'm not disturbing you." She let him in.

They went into a large room, also white. They stood there for a few minutes while he told her something about what had gone wrong in his son's life. Then he put his hand on her breast. They made love. They talked about getting married. Aunt Marion came in with a wedding dress and veil. She was accompanied by deliverymen who carried flowers. The house changed into a church: the wedding was about to begin. But Roy wasn't there. In his place stood his child, Eric. Aunt Marion was at her side; she seemed to think everything was normal. So did everybody else. And she, Sandra, was the bride—she was there to get married. She took Eric's hand. She said, "I do." He said, "Sure, I guess so." Then they were going back down the aisle together. Everyone else was happy; some of them were even applauding. But she felt defrauded. She didn't see why she hadn't been able to get the one she'd wanted. "Where is he?" she asked her aunt, who said, "He's on a tropical island."

The next morning was a sunny day. A light, springlike breeze fluttered across the neighborhood gardens and twirled back on itself, playing. She felt it on her face when she opened the front door to take in the newspaper.

She made herself some real coffee and had a large, thick piece of toast with butter and honey. The bread was from a homebaked loaf—the kind of thing that was probably as fattening as cake. She put extra milk in her coffee. She didn't turn on the radio or the television, or bother to open the paper. The only sounds to be heard were of her chewing and swallowing. It seemed as if the rest of the world had disappeared. She wondered suddenly why her aunt didn't have a pet. Dogs could be too much trouble: you had to walk them and they pined if you left them. But a cat wouldn't mind being left on its own, or being fed and patted by strangers. She thought that she might give her aunt a kitten. She'd have to find out first, whether it would be a good idea. There were many people, more than you'd think, who didn't like pets, and who believed that life with a pet carried the same demands and responsibilities as life with another person.

She went for a walk. She stepped out of the door and into a world that seemed to be abandoned by the human race. The birds were still there and a lone dog trotted purposefully, tail-up, in the distance. But no people came into view, not even children. Everyone must have listened to the weather report, considered it believable, and decided to drive away to other places: to see friends, to visit relatives, to search for the more beautifully leaved trees that must be somewhere, although no one had seen them that year: any place, different but the same.

She started out in the direction of the pioneer statue. Her feet, her whole body felt light and unusually flexible. A wonderful day could really be better than people.

The road she was walking along led her through a neighborhood where the houses were small, as were their front yards, but there was no indication of poverty. On the contrary, houses and gardens alike were well tended. Aunt Marion would have lived in such an area if she'd moved into a house forty years later than she had. When she'd married, these houses wouldn't have been where they were. They came after the days of large families.

Two turnings brought her down to the end of a long road that, as far as she could guess, curved back towards where she'd hoped—the day before—to find the statue. When she got to the point where she expected to see the beginnings of the road she remembered, there were three branches: one kept on, the other turned off down a hill and the third seemed to go back in the right direction, but uphill and at an angle that, if unchanged, might lead her eventually to the other side of town. She was lost again. She was also getting tired.

Where had she made the mistake? Or had she taken more than one wrong turning? She stood still for a minute, thinking that there was no way of guessing which way the roads went, especially for someone with such a poor sense of direction.

As she was looking ahead and to the right, she noticed smoke coming from somewhere. At least one person was at home and out in the gardens around her, burning leaves. The smell was faint, and gone away, back again and then lost. It might be coming from a long way off. At that moment a man appeared in the road that ran from the top of the hill. She turned around. She decided to retrace her steps. It wasn't exactly that she felt nervous, but she didn't know the neighborhood, nobody else was nearby, and the locality from which the stranger came was unknown; he was therefore to be avoided, whereas if she had seen a man raking leaves in a yard, she'd have gone up to him and asked how to get back to the street her aunt's house was on. A man standing by his own house was fixed, identifiable and as safe as if he were wearing a nametag. Strangers could come from anywhere. She forgot that she too was a stranger.

She was almost at the end of the row of houses and approaching another fork in the road—hoping that she'd remember it—when she heard someone calling her name from behind her. She turned. The man from the top of the hill was coming up to her at a slow run. She didn't recognize him until he called her name again and waved. It was Roy, Eric's father, from the night before. He looked different. He was wearing a pullover and a pair of chinos. He might have been a student or even a teenager.

"Hi," he said. "I waved at you from back there."

"I didn't see," she said. "I was trying to figure out what road to take. I'm lost."

"This one goes back to your house."

"I wanted to get to the statue of the pioneer woman."

"Oh. Sure. Wilhelmina."

"Is that her name?"

"No, that's just what we call her."

We? Did that mean him and his son, or him and the wife he was divorced from? Or a new girl he was going out with?

"It's a long walk up the hill," he said, "or back to Trellis Road, and then you jog left."

"That's where I went wrong."

"I'll walk you back." He started to move forward, putting his hand on her arm for a moment as he did so. She fell into step beside him.

"It's a beautiful day," she said.

"One of the few. It's been a lousy year. Even now: I hear it's still raining just about everyplace else."

"Well, I guess we need it, after the drought. The trees look so sad."

"Yes. Everything looks wrong."

They passed a yard where someone had been burning a pile of leaves. Whoever it was had gone back inside.

"How's Eric?" she said.

"He's okay. Quiet. It follows a pattern. I guess you've seen him around here before. He's been going off like this for— oh, a year and some. Usually he comes home of his own accord."

"Oh?"

"It's hard to know what to do. I keep hoping he'll grow out of it."

"Have you asked a doctor about it?"

"He doesn't need a doctor. He needs a mother."

"Well," she said, "he's got one, hasn't he?"

"What he had was worse than having nothing."

"There's something I ought to tell you."

"Yes?"

"He threatened me with a knife."

"Oh, God. I've always thought most of what he does is for show. And a lot of talk."

"I don't know how serious it was. The knife was just an ordinary table knife. But it could have been a sharper one. He yelled at me not to phone you and he held it like this. Right? I couldn't tell if he meant to do anything, because I don't know him. But it's a bad sign. Especially since—well, at the moment he's too young to be dangerous. But what's going to happen later? He's smart and he doesn't like people."

"He likes you."

"Oh? But I'm the one who betrayed him. I handed him over to you."

"I guess you made him realize that it was necessary."

They came to the point where the neighborhood changed. She saw that there was a road running around to the back of one of the houses; she hadn't noticed it, and if she had, she'd have assumed it to be a private driveway. Now that she was seeing from another angle, she remembered that it was the road to the statue. "We're here," she said. "This is it."

"Do you want to go see it?"

She looked at her watch. "I'd like to," she said, "but I don't know what time my aunt—she said she'd be back on Sunday afternoon. That could mean one minute past twelve."

"That's a long way off."

"Yes. Okay, sure. I'd like to." They walked up the road she'd missed. He talked about the neighborhood: he'd moved there around the time when he was at college. He said, "So you live with your family? That's nice. Hardly anyone does any more."

"Oh, I don't, either. I live in town. I'm only keeping an eye on my aunt's house while she's away for the weekend."

"In that case, it was incredibly lucky that you were there."

"I don't know about that."

"Oh yes—definitely. Ricky doesn't respond to everyone. In fact, he'll hardly speak to anyone. I think he sort of opened up to you. He keeps talking about you."

"What does he say?"

"How nice you are."

"Well. I was just thinking last night that my great-aunt would have handled the whole thing a lot better. I don't know much about children."

"Christ, who does? They seem to do certain things at set ages, so there's a general standard you can measure their behavior against, but that only works if you've got one of those so-called average children. I'll tell you one thing: the worst advice you can get about them comes from people who are supposed to make their living out of it. Teachers and those behavior people. Especially when they're faced with a boy like Ricky. Aside from everything else, he's simply a lot more intelligent than any of his teachers. And the ones who can see it, don't like that. Most of them are too dumb to register. They've got a format that somebody's handed them, and they go ahead and shove until every child's been squeezed into it. They tried to do the same with me. Of course, he's not helping things. I think about a year ago he figured out that there's just about nothing they can do to you, if you refuse to cooperate. I wasn't smart enough to get that far until I was in my teens. And by that time I wanted all the things I was being bribed with. He doesn't want anything. He's got nothing to lose. Oh, hell. I'm sorry to dump all this on you, especially on such a fantastic day. Look at that."

They'd reached the top of the hill, from which further

wooded lands—in front and to the sides—stretched away. If the trees had been in their normal autumn colors the sight would have been staggering. Even as it was, the air glittered, houses to the far distance were picked out crisply; you could see right back to the next town, miles away.

"Not bad," he said.

"It's wonderful. I only saw it like this once before, when I was in school." She looked down on the roadways ahead. They were laid out as clearly as if on a map. Although she couldn't see the statue, she could make out the spot where it stood, among evergreens. When she turned back to him she knew that while she'd been absorbed in the view, he'd been looking at her. On his face she caught the last of the expression that had been there: concentrated, possessive. It made her self-conscious; she wanted to move on. "It's over there, isn't it?" she said.

He nodded. They began to stroll to the fork in the road.

"Maybe," she said, "you could find one of those schools for gifted children, where he'd be able to meet other kids and teachers that didn't make him feel so bored and out of step."

"I could. It would mean sending him away. I don't want to do that. Unless he starts asking about it himself. That might happen in a few years. That would be great. But so far, I figure: He's been rejected by one parent—I don't want him to get the idea that the one he's got left is trying to get rid of him, too. Poor little squirt. I was just the same at his age."

"You?" She couldn't believe that a man who looked so open, athletic, handsome and successful, had ever been anything other than a miniature version of what he was at the moment.

"Just exactly," he said. "I thought they started off, right at the beginning, thinking I was a freak. It didn't seem to me that they were doing anything to help. Or that they wanted to. It takes a long while to understand that there's not really much you can do when a child's unhappiness is caused by not fitting in. You've either got to grow out of it, or move away."

They came to a second turning. The road started to go downhill. Soon they were surrounded by fir trees. She said, "He could become a member of one of those groups for people with high IQs."

"He's done that already. They all have endless games with each other. Playing chess on the computer and doing those wargames where you conquer the world."

"He likes those computer things?"

"Sure. So do I. It's part of my work."

"Oh? He said your job was doing the advertising for toys."

He stopped walking, and laughed. He said, "That's one way of putting it, I suppose. I'm in aeronautics. What else did he say?"

"Oh, lots of things."

"Such as?"

"Maybe he wouldn't like it if I repeated them."

"You're kidding. I'm his father."

"I'll tell you something: I can remember a family Christmas, when I was about five, and one of my grown-up relatives teased me about something I'd put on my letter to Santa Claus. I was just mortified. Everybody else was fine—they didn't say a thing. But it only takes one. So, I know that children can be funny, but sometimes they just don't hide what they think. And that's not really funny. It's—"

"It's just artless. Without guile."

"Right. So to get together and laugh about something that might be a secret dream somebody told you in private—you see what I mean?"

"Of course," he said.

"You're laughing."

"I'm wondering what you asked for."

To the left, beyond him, she saw the break in the trees. She skipped towards it. He followed. The statue stood at the end of a narrow path lined with plants that had flowered earlier in the year. Only the green showed now. She hadn't remembered them, nor the enclosing height of the pines and hemlocks, nor the fact that the statue itself, up on a plinth, was so small.

"It looks different," she said. "I don't remember those lines of flowers or anything."

"How old were you the last time you saw it?"

"The only time. About eleven, nearly twelve."

"That might explain it."

"But I was almost as tall as I am now."

"Well, the flowers have been there for six years. And the trees would have grown. And you only saw it once."

"Oh, I like it just as much now, but I don't like the idea that I could remember something all wrong. Why should that be?"

"You've fitted it in with the other things you've seen since."

"I see." The statue hadn't changed; she had. She liked that idea even less than the thought of being wrong. If you weren't what you were, what were you? Who were you?

"It's a pretty little statue," he said.

"Yes. And I like the story. It's supposed to be true, too, although I never heard if she got back to her family afterwards, or even whether or not she found her husband."

"That's not important. In all those stories the main thing is the endeavor. If you're going to wonder about reality, none of it makes sense."

"Why not?"

"I bet they'd have given her a rough time in the locker rooms."

"She wouldn't have had to be in a regiment. And they wouldn't have been in barracks, anyway. They were all out in the woods."

"Until she got to some kind of a town where she could get information about her husband. As soon as she came into contact with other people, she'd be eating with them and washing with them."

"They always leave that out of the history books."

"Because it's assumed. That's like not making a movie that's got people taking a leak all the time. You know they do, but there's no reason to put it in unless that's your favorite part of the story."

"Why do you call her Wilhelmina?"

"I can't even remember. Had enough?"

"Yes. Thank you for showing me how to get here."

"My pleasure. I'll walk you home."

They walked back slowly. She asked him about his work. He wanted to know if she'd seen a play he'd read about; and, if not, would she like to go to it with him? She said that she would. She wrote down the address and phone number of her place in town. She asked what day of the week he had in mind. "Tomorrow," he said.

• • •

AUNT MARION didn't arrive till nightfall. She was loaded down with packages and was full of apologies for her lateness. "It was such a beautiful day," she said.

"How was Elsie?"

"Much better—almost transformed. We had a lovely day. We talked all about old times. You know, it makes such a difference, when you reach my age, to know people who remember you the way you were as a child. And they remember your parents and grandparents, too. I used to think that remark of Will Rogers's was so stupid, but sometimes nowadays I wonder if it mightn't be true, as long as you had enough time to get to know the person. Time does seem to give you the truth in ways that are hard to explain. I think about it a lot."

"What's all the shopping?"

"Bargains, dear. I've spent a fortune. Elsie decided that we'd go out as soon as I got there. I didn't think she looked well at all. I thought we ought to stay at home. But she wouldn't take no for an answer. A very stubborn woman when she wants to be. She took me out to one of those enormous shopping malls. But it wasn't like any one I've ever seen. The quality of the merchandise—I was bowled over. And they had a sale on. We ripped through that place like nobody's business. Wait till I show you."

"Aunt Marion, I had a strange thing happen while you were away."

"Not the pipes?"

"No, it—"

"Or something electrical?"

"Nothing like that. The house is fine. And so is the windowpane they delivered. And everything else. No. It was a little boy, who rang the doorbell and seemed to be lost. I asked him in and he started telling me all kinds of wild stories. And then he asked me if there was anything to eat, so I took him into the kitchen. And I'm afraid he's eaten up just about everything in the refrigerator."

"Good. That's what it was for."

"I thought I was never going to get rid of him, but then his father came looking for him and the boy finally agreed to go back. They live around here; I wonder if you know them? His name's Roy Martinson. The Roy stands for Conroy."

"Oh," Aunt Marion said. "It rings a bell. Faintly. You'll have to let me think. I've been back in my schooldays all weekend." She bustled around, found some bread and a few cookies that Eric hadn't discovered, and made tea. Over their meal she showed Sandra the haul from her shopping binge: shoes, gloves, a tweed skirt, yards of summer materials. "I never used to like shopping," she said. "It was always a duty —a necessity. And I had to be careful with the pennies. I used to walk miles to find something that cost a little less. That was a long time ago. The world has changed for the better in that way. Money has changed. These credit cards . . . Of course, we were brought up to think that that sort of thing was immoral: to be in debt. And I'd never dream of letting it mount up—I send my check off straight away. But it's nice to go on a spree with an old friend."

"To buy things you don't really need, but you want them like crazy because they're pretty."

"Yes. And even to spend a while looking at things that you'd never bother with. We went to a camera store. That was very interesting. I thought that—for what they were—the prices were quite reasonable. I've still got Hudson's old camera, but he used to make it sound so complicated that I was sort of tempted by these new ones. They do everything for you. Ordinary people never used to be able to work mechanical gadgets without a lot of training. Nowadays you just buy a box and push the buttons and out comes something—like magic. We went into a typewriter shop too, because Elsie wanted to sit down and I thought I'd like to find out about word processors. It's so embarrassing to say that you only came in because you couldn't walk another step. They were very kind. They found Elsie a chair straight away and a nice young man explained the machines to me. Naturally I wouldn't have taken up his time if they'd been busy in there, but everyone else seemed to be down at the china reject shop. They had a clearance sale on."

"But you didn't buy any?"

"We didn't want to carry anything heavy. And besides, what would I do with one more earthenware pot or a willow-pattern coffee cup? Most of my things just stay in the cupboard until the bridge-club meetings. No. We thought about going into the garden center, but by that time we were getting hungry, so we stopped for lunch. My, the different restaurants they have: there's a whole place just for desserts. It's called "Sweet Stuff." They serve everything you can name. Then there's a restaurant for breakfast, and a teashop and all kinds of international food: Chinese, Indian, Malayan, Swiss, Italian, Hungarian. Well, we couldn't make up our minds. We went into the nearest one."

"Aunt Marion, I think you've hit on a new system for fun shopping: only go into a store if you have to sit down."

"It worked very well, I must admit. They gave us a really nice luncheon."

"What did you have?"

"A salad full of radish sprouts. And for dessert, a peanut-butter waffle with something called Dreme Whip. Delicious. It almost convinced me that I ought to buy myself a waffle iron. But I wouldn't use it enough. Do you have one?"

"No. For the same reason. We had one at home. It just sat there, except for about once a year. We used to get it out around Christmastime. I think nobody ever wanted to have to clean it afterwards."

"And Elsie had a most intriguing soup: carrot soup with cardamum, ginger and a bit of cream. I meant to write that down."

Sandra stood up. She crossed the kitchen and picked a pencil out of the flat straw basket on the windowsill behind the sink. She tore a piece of paper off the notepad next to the basket.

"Thank you, dear," her aunt said. "I owe one or two people a good recipe. That spinach and cottage cheese casserole was the last surefire thing I had to trade with. I hope it wasn't too dull for you here."

"No. There was that little boy."

"Oh, yes. Of course."

"And I went for a couple of walks and watched a nature movie on TV. And then I did a lot of thinking about that boyfriend. You know."

"And?"

"I decided that I've got to break it off. I don't know why I let it go on so long. He's always going away on those hunting weekends or taking a trip to see some team play a game. The only time we're together is when we're eating or going to the movies."

"Men do have their particular interests, you know. They like to get together every once in a while, to drink and tell stories. It's like my bridge meetings. I'd miss them dreadfully."

"That isn't all of it. I'm not having any fun. And he doesn't even know I'm there." He just wanted someone to sleep with. She didn't think her aunt would care to hear that; it would make plain what Sandra's relationship with men was, and the idea would offend her. Aunt Marion undoubtedly knew all those things in any case, but she appreciated a certain amount of tact: they weren't actually to be mentioned.

"If you don't enjoy his company," Aunt Marion said, "then I'd do what they recommend on the stockmarket. I'd cut my losses."

"That's what I'm going to do."

"Well, then. I'm glad to hear that your weekend hasn't been a waste."

"On the contrary. I really think I needed a little time away from things."

She went upstairs and checked that she'd packed everything. She put on her jacket and brought her bag down. At the door she kissed her aunt goodbye, stepped out and turned around again, to smile and wave.

The old woman stood holding the door. Her face was thoughtful. She told Sandra to have a good trip back to town, and to drive carefully. Then she said, "Oh. I know what it was: Conroy Martinson. I remember now. He's the one who killed his wife."

● ● ●

SOMEHOW, although Aunt Marion seldom got things wrong, she must have mixed up one story with another. Sandra was so sure of it that she hadn't contradicted her, nor did she remember, until she was well into the weekend's homecoming rush of cars, that there was evidence to back up her conviction: both father and son had spoken of the ex-wife in the present tense. She was certainly still alive. Sandra put the matter from her mind and concentrated on the increasing traffic.

When she got home, she was later than she'd thought she would be. She dropped her bag inside the door. She looked around. Not even a new coat of paint would cheer the place up. She'd lived there too long and she'd never liked it.

Her eye fell on one of Bert's knapsacks. His hockey stick and fishing rod were in the closet, the iceskates and baseball bat in the cupboard under the window. It was just luck that everyone in the building had been issued a new set of keys after the Huxtables had had the burglary; and that she hadn't yet made copies for Bert. She gathered all his clothes and equipment into a pile near the door. Then she climbed into bed and finished reading her novel.

In the morning, she bundled Bert's possessions into the car. She drove to work early so that she could dump everything with his secretary before he came in.

The moment she walked away from his office, she felt elated. She crossed to the other side of the building, took the elevator down and went to her desk. She picked up the phone and made an appointment to get her hair done during her lunch hour. On the dot of one she left her desk, beating her friend, Maureen, to the doorway into the hall.

At the hairdresser's they gave her a sandwich and a cup of coffee. While she was trying to balance the cup and get it up to her mouth without hitting the hood of the dryer, she noticed that another woman was having the same sort of trouble, but worse: she hadn't figured out that she should leave the saucer and spoon behind.

On her way back to the office she ran into Bert. "Sandra. Hi," he said.

"Hi," she answered. She kept walking.

"Where are you going?"

"Back to work."

"I thought we'd go out to lunch."

"I've just had lunch."

"I mean: I did think. Where were you?"

"Hairdresser. Bert, I'm going to be late."

"I thought maybe we could have a talk."

"About what?"

"I'll drop by tonight, okay?"

"No, not tonight."

"Why not?"

"Because I can't. Come on, Bert. What do you want to tell me?"

"Well, I've been thinking: Maybe we should cool it for a while."

"That's not enough."

"What?"

"We've got to admit that it's no good, and say goodbye."

"I didn't mean anything drastic like that."

"Well, I do. That's why I left all your stuff with your secretary. Didn't she tell you?"

"Oh. She did mention something. I thought it must have

been those spiked running shoes I asked you to get fixed."

"I'll phone you at the weekend," she said.

"Hell, Sandra, you know I can't this weekend."

"Okay. Next weekend."

"What's wrong with tomorrow night?"

"I can't. I could see you some day for lunch, I guess."

He pulled out an appointment book. She started to walk ahead. She got as far as the steps in front of the glass doors. "How about Thursday?" he called after her. She nodded, waved and went inside. She had no intention of keeping the date. She still felt irritated, which was silly. There was no point in being angry because she'd let things between them go on too long. Now she begrudged him the time she'd spent in his company, yet that wasn't his fault. It was hers. Everything would be different when she went to the theater with Roy.

That afternoon she was out of the office in record time and on her way home to get ready for the evening.

HE ARRIVED on the dot of six. And he was driving the kind of car that looked like the ones you could see in races. It was red. He said, "I hope you don't mind riding low to the ground."

"As long as we don't drive under a truck," she said. She buckled up her seatbelt. She felt as if she were in a fighter plane, next to the controls.

On their way in to town they passed small groups of children dressed up as witches, ghosts and goblins. A few of the gangs included a grown woman: a mother who was too worried about her children to allow them out trick-or-treating even if they were surrounded by friends. When Sandra had been at school, they hadn't allowed that kind of thing. If anyone tried to bring a mother along, or even an older brother or sister, the original crowd would go into a huddle, plan out what moves to make and then, at a signal, run out on the sissy and the protector.

He drove to an underground parking lot that belonged to a hotel up the road from the theater. The attendant knew him; he also knew the car; an expression of intense compassion poured over his face as he got behind the wheel to park it.

They went into the building at a side entrance. There didn't seem to be any guests, and only a few of the staff were working. Over at the reception desk a white-haired man was reading a ledger. Roy walked her across the lobbies and into a waiting room. "I love this place," he said. "It used to be a grand old hotel back in the nineties. Everybody used to come here. Then—I don't know what happened. Maybe they didn't modernize the bathrooms, or something. I've never stayed here, so I don't know what it's like upstairs. People used to come here in the thirties for a while. That was the last time it was fashionable. It's a shame. When I was at college across the river, it was just as empty as it is tonight. I used to bring my friends over for cocktails. But everybody was trying to be casual then: eating hamburgers and wearing sneakers. It never caught on with anyone else."

He took her into the bar and introduced her to a gnomelike old bartender whose name was Perkins. He and Perkins talked about the hotel, the staff and old clients, while Sandra gazed around the room, taking in the immensely high ceiling, the marble floors, the thick, flower-patterned rugs, the old furniture that was solid but elegant.

"Nice?" Roy asked her.

She nodded. Already she liked the things he liked.

They had two of Perkins's secret-recipe cocktails. Sandra would have liked a third, or even more. She'd have liked to sit there for hours. But Roy looked at his watch. It was time to go.

They caught a cab to the theater and arrived in time to look through the program. "I haven't been to see a play in years," she said.

"At the last play I went to, I was surrounded by people who kept whispering to each other all the time."

"That's because of television. It gets to be automatic."

"I was ready to start hitting them over the head."

"They wouldn't have noticed. They're those people who turn on the machine and talk over it all day long."

The light dimmed slowly. The chattering of the audience gave way to a hush. As the house lights went out altogether, the curtain rose on a scene set in a psychoanalyst's office. The analyst was pretending to listen to a patient, yet all the while he was doing everything in his power to prevent a woman, hidden behind his chair, from stepping out and revealing herself. She was trying to leave the office. And she was also attempting to put on the rest of her clothes. The patient talked about how he thought that his wife might be seeing another man.

The next scene was set in the office of a female analyst. She had once been married to the first analyst and now she was taking notes while she listened to one of her patients.

Each new scene allowed the audience to see that the characters who confessed their infidelities or doubts were giving information to the very people who were involved in their betrayal. Not only that: after the initial misunderstandings had been shown, they were followed by variations; the characters who appeared to be the conscious manipulators of the first scenes became the unwitting victims of those that followed. And after the second act the pace quickened: people were rushing through doors and dashing behind sofas so fast that every person on stage was suffering from at least four mistaken ideas. But it all worked out in the end: by the time the final curtain came down, all the couples—even the two analysts—were reunited, and everything was serene and reasonable, with only a slight loose end announcing that perhaps a gentle tweak at the plot could start the whole mix-up all over again.

Sandra and Roy turned to smile at each other while they applauded. Before the last curtain call he took her hand and led her out of her seat to follow the couple next to him, who were heading down the center aisle.

They were out on the street, with their coats on, and climbing into a taxi before the main crowd had left the auditorium. And soon they were sitting at a table for two, in a restaurant where the lighting was only slightly dimmed and the waiters and the other customers were lively enough to make the place fun.

They talked about the play: how delightful it had been and how cleverly it managed to string the audience along from one point to the next. The action had been like clockwork—like one of those watches where you could look in and see the wheels going around. Cause and effect had been so clearly demonstrated: you began to think that if only you could pin down the sources of your own mistakes and confusions, they too would be explained and, consequently, solved.

They ate and drank and looked into each other's eyes. He told her stories about where he'd grown up. She talked—because he asked her—about Aunt Marion and then about the rest of her relatives: her attractive, pig-headed sister, her maddening and sometimes unkind, yet irresistible, mother, her adorable, absent-minded father, who was the peacemaker of the family.

All at once she realized that she'd had a lot to drink. She didn't want to spoil things; she put her glass down. "This is a nice place," she said.

"Yes, it's not bad. At least the food's all right. And you can see what you're eating. And nobody's playing a piano right in your ear."

"Is Eric out in a costume tonight?"

"He said he didn't want to. He said he'd decided that Halloween was for the younger kids."

"I always loved it. I was very upset when it all stopped. Who's with him?"

"Somebody named Karen."

"Not the one who gives him a bath?"

"He told you about that?"

"She didn't sound like a very good babysitter."

"No, but she's a great cook. That's what I hired her for. Her name's Debbie."

"Oh. He didn't say she worked for you. I got the idea that she came in from outside."

"That's Ricky. He'll take something that's basically true, extract the part that made the impression on him and re-work it so that it's completely different. Something's there that's similar to what was in the actual event, but even if you dig for it, the emphasis is all wrong."

"I sort of figured that out while he was talking to me. But I think most people do all that anyway, don't you? I do it. To make myself more interesting, or to impress. Most of the time I'm not really aware of doing it."

"He's fully aware of what he's doing, I can tell you that. Don't ever underestimate his intelligence."

"He needs some friends," she said. She cleared her throat and added, "At least, that's the way it seemed to me."

"Uh-huh."

"Because he needed to talk."

"I don't think it's because the other kids avoid him. But I don't know what comes first: he's standoffish with them. And a snob. They call him names. And then he says something back, full of five-syllable words they can't find in the dictionary because they don't know how to spell them. That's how the business with Schizo began: because he used the term 'schizophrenic' in class. It was one of the words he was showing off with; he'd even named his pet hamster Schizo, because of the way it ran around. The hamster—that was horrible. Of course he didn't mean to do it. And it taught him something he'll always remember, but still—I'll never forget that moment when he came screaming down the stairs, all covered in blood."

"What happened?"

"Oh, he . . . he's so smart, you know. It's hard to remember that sometimes he just doesn't see things any idiot can understand."

"What happened?" she said again.

"He cut it open, to see what was inside."

"Oh, no." She put down her fork.

"I don't think the blood bothered him at all. It was when the hamster started to squeak. Then he was terrified."

She put a hand over her face. She couldn't get rid of the picture; Eric and his hamster: cutting it open with a razor blade, or something less grown-up—a pair of scissors, maybe.

"He was so upset about it that he cried for hours. We held a funeral for it and everything. Buried it in a shoebox, underneath a lilac bush in the back yard. I was just beginning to believe that he'd recovered, when he started to talk about how some people were vegetarians because they thought it was wrong to kill animals. I worked for days on explaining the difference between a domestic pet and an animal bred for consumption."

"Is there a difference?"

"Of course there is. That's why farmers eat the animals their neighbors sell, and let them buy the ones they've raised. It's the emotion you invest in them."

"It isn't the act of killing?"

"You're not a vegetarian."

"No. But if I had to kill the animals, I would be. So would a lot of people."

"Not me."

"And Eric? Ricky?"

"I think he'd agree with you. On the other hand, if it were for something like medical research, I have a feeling he'd be able to kill anything or anybody without giving a thought to how much it hurt. He's good at putting things in different compartments. That's another reason why I have such a hard time keeping up with him. He's always got something new."

"Well, he's still growing." She changed the subject back to the play. They had coffee and a liqueur.

It was still fairly warm outside, in spite of the late hour and the time of year. They walked back to the hotel. As he started the car he said, "I've always wanted to check in here for the night sometime, just for fun." He looked at her as he said it.

"I can see why," she said quickly, brushing aside the suggestion he'd put in front of her. She knew it was intended and he knew that she knew, but she had to act as if she hadn't seen what he'd meant. The whole thing was ridiculous but they were supposed to follow a prescribed set of moves in the correct order, otherwise the result would be like a painting-by-number game where no one had obeyed the instructions. Unlike her meeting with Eric, there was a particular, formulated method according to which this encounter was meant to proceed, and to finish.

"It's a great hotel," she said. "It's one of those places you know you'll want to go back to."

At the street entrance of the building she lived in he said, "I'll see you to your door."

At the door he kissed her. It wasn't an ordinary kiss. She was ready to give him everything right then, but she'd never said yes on the first date, not even when she'd been a little drunk. She pulled away. He whispered, "No?"

"It isn't that I don't want to," she said.

"Can I see you tomorrow? Same time, same place?"

"All right. Yes," she said.

She closed the door slowly. If they went out the next night and came back to the apartment afterwards . . . She suddenly thought: It was going to take her all night to clean the place up.

She put the books and papers into neat stacks, dragged the second table back to where it was supposed to be and hid the laundrybags behind the bathroom door. She was dusting the top shelf of the bookcase when the downstairs doorbell rang.

She picked up the receiver of the entryphone and said hello. There was no answer. She said hello again. A man's voice, not easy to recognize, said, "I forgot something." It was Bert. It had to be, even though it didn't sound like his voice.

"It's late," she said. "Phone me tomorrow. Goodnight." She hung up. She put the chain on the door.

The bell went again. She ignored it. She went back to cleaning the apartment. The bell rang steadily, and insistently, for nearly a minute; then there was silence. She finished everything but the vacuuming, working fast, and got ready for bed. Before she turned in for the night she took out the phone book and telephoned the twenty-four-hour locksmiths. She asked them to come change a lock for her at six in the morning.

She dropped into bed. It seemed to her afterwards that she had many dark and fragmented dreams but she couldn't remember any of them. She felt that the alarm had rung just a little before it was quite fair. When the locksmith arrived she was already dressed and drinking coffee.

He didn't tell her his name. Over the entryphone he just said, "Locksmith," and at her door he told her, "From Lockett's Locks."

She offered him a cup of coffee; he said that that was okay, it wouldn't take long. "Been burgled?" he asked.

"No."

"Well, that's something, anyways."

"Um."

"Lost your keys?"

"No, I lent a set to somebody. And now it sort of makes me nervous."

"Better be safe," he told her.

"Right. I guess most of your work is for people who've had their keys stolen."

"All kinds of reasons. Divorce—we get a lot of that. And some people change their keys every time they get the workmen in to fix something. It's a never-ending job. Twenty-four hours, like the ad says." When he'd finished, he gave her two keys.

She put one of the keys in the bottom desk drawer and the other on her keychain. She threw the old key into the wastebasket so that she wouldn't mix it up with one of the others.

Twenty minutes after the locksmith had left, Bert was outside the door. He'd persuaded, or tricked, some other tenant into buzzing the street door for him. He was trying to work the lock with his old key.

She stepped up to the door, put the chain back on and said, "Who is it?"

"It's me."

She opened the door as far as the chain allowed. She said, "Go away, Bert. I've had the lock changed."

"Who was that guy?" he asked.

"What guy?"

"I saw you go out with him last night. You know. The one with the incredible car."

"What do you want, Bert?"

"I want to talk to you. Is he in there? Come on, Sandra. Open up."

"Nobody's here, Bert. Will you please go away?"

"I'm not going anywhere till you let me in."

"No. I won't. And why should I? If you don't let me close this door, I'll phone the police. I mean it."

"All right," he said. "All right." He took his foot away. "What the hell? What do you think I'm going to do to you? If there wasn't anybody here last night, why wouldn't you let me in?"

"If I'd let you in, I'd never have been able to get you to go away again."

"Oh, I'd have gone. I'm not one of those violent types. You know me."

"I know how much you weigh. And I could just see you flopping down on the couch and talking at me for six hours about how I should have second thoughts. If you didn't want to leave, I wouldn't be able to throw you out."

"Oh, come on."

"I've got to go," she told him. She closed the door.

She had time to do the vacuuming, wash two pairs of tights and get a load of laundry hung up over the bathtub before she went to work.

There was a note on her desk to say that she was supposed to get in touch with Bert as soon as she got in. She didn't. Fifteen minutes later, when she was about to go to her first meeting, his secretary called. Sandra was ready with an excuse, but he came in on the line before she could get it out.

"You can't keep this up," he told her. "I've got work to do. I'll see you for lunch."

"I don't want lunch," she said. "I'm out for dinner tonight." He'd already hung up.

Five minutes before she was due to go to lunch, she

scooted around to the back of the building, took the janitor's elevator and went out one of the emergency doors. The only difficulty left was the open stretch between the front of the building and the main road. If she hurried, she could walk all around the block and try to approach the shops from the far side. Of course she didn't need to buy herself any lunch at all. There was a coffee-and-sandwich machine down the hall from her office. There were lots of them, all through the building. But if she stayed at her desk, Bert would probably come in and make some big outburst—or, at the least, a loud complaint—right there.

As soon as she'd crossed the double main road, she thought that she was in the clear. Everything was going to be fine. She slowed down and looked around: another nice day. She wondered where he'd take her tonight. Perhaps nothing would happen. But if it did? And maybe the dark blue taffeta wasn't right. She'd have to iron the gray dress.

As she turned in to the alleyway between the row of shops where the hairdresser's was and the arcade that she was headed for, Bert grabbed her elbow. He said, "Look, we've got to talk about this. You can't just start going out with somebody else. What am I supposed to do?"

She pulled her arm back. "I don't know," she said. "That's up to you. I told you yesterday: there's nothing to talk about. No fuss, no bother, no more Sandra. I should have done it a long time ago, but I was under the impression that we were engaged. I can't believe it now."

"But we are. I mean, we're going to get married, aren't we?"

"You've never mentioned it. And the only time I ever tried

to get you to say something about it, you told me we shouldn't rush things."

"Well, I always sort of assumed that it was going to happen. I mean, we love each other and everything."

"Bert, you don't even like me."

"What the hell is that supposed to mean?"

"No. You want to go out with your friends and have a good time. And somebody like your mother will be back at home, waiting to clean the mud off your hiking boots. It isn't just that we've got different interests."

"You could come along whenever you like. Why don't you?"

"I guess I would have if you'd ever asked me. You've always made me feel that I'd spoil things if I went along and slowed you down. Maybe I would have. But we could have done other things. We could just have taken a walk together every once in a while."

"Where are you going? It's this way. I made a reservation at Francesco's."

"I'm just going to have a sandwich someplace."

"You can fit in a plate of spaghetti. Come on. I'm hungry."

"Well, I'm not. I'm out to dinner tonight, with lots of food and wine. I don't want a hot lunch."

"You're going out to some big candlelit seduction scene? Jesus, Sandra. What are you trying to do to me?"

"I'm saying goodbye. Why can't you admit that you don't really mind?"

"That's not true."

"You mind that I've done it first, that's all."

He started to wave his arms and talk about how she'd never

given him any sign—not one, not a hint—that she'd been unhappy with the way things were. And this just wasn't fair.

She'd tried, she said, she honestly had. Every time she'd opened her mouth to tell him, he was in the middle of watching a football game, or ice hockey or baseball or basketball. All she'd ever been able to get out of him was uh-huh and uh-uh. And now her lunch hour was nearly over and she was starving.

She turned right around and ran. As fast as she could, she raced down the alleyway, out to the sidewalk, across the street, along the arcade and into the little sandwich shop where she sometimes went with Maureen. She sat down at the first empty table she could see. A waitress came up to her straight away. Sandra said, "A tunafish sandwich on rye, please."

"With lettuce?"

Over the girl's shoulder Sandra saw Bert come bolting in through the door. "With lettuce," she said, "but I think maybe I'd better make that an order to go."

"We don't do food to go."

"Okay. In that case, could you make it fast, please?"

Bert yanked away one of the empty chairs and sat down next to her. "I'm not leaving it like this," he announced. Three people turned to look.

"Are you together?" the waitress asked.

"No," Sandra answered.

Bert said yes.

"What can I get you?"

"Roast beef, rare. Sliced thin. White bread. Mustard, pickles."

"You want that with potato chips?"

"Sure."

Sandra started to slide out of her chair. If she made a dash for it, she might be able to get out on to the street before he'd understood her actions.

She took a quick step forward. He shot to his feet and grabbed her around the waist. "You stay right there," he ordered. Everyone was looking now.

He pushed her back down into her chair. "And two black coffees," he told the waitress.

"I'll have some milk in mine," Sandra muttered.

"Oh yeah, I forgot."

Her eyes moistened with anger and affection: he still couldn't remember anything about her—what she liked or didn't like, where her parents went in the summer, what her sister's name was. But he was sweet; insensitive, but straightforward. And he was willing to follow her into a strange, small place and make an embarrassing show of himself in order to stop her from leaving him. If she'd crawled under one of the tables, he'd have gone after her. Of course she was still fond of him. That was undeniable. She wasn't going to forget him. But she wouldn't be able to stand living with him for the rest of her life.

She put her hand on his arm and said, "I don't want to argue. I've got somebody else, that's all." She looked at him steadily.

He said, "But it isn't serious. It can't be."

She nodded. She took away her hand.

"Well," he said. "Well."

They sat there in silence for a few moments. She'd lost her appetite. She wanted to get out.

The waitress came with their food. Bert lifted his sandwich. He said, "Maybe you need some time to think about things."

"Bert, I have thought."

"Get it out of your system, sort of. That kind of idea. I guess I took a lot of things for granted."

"You want me to try it out with somebody else and then come back if it doesn't work?"

"Well, I don't like it. But if it's what you need? You'll find out: he doesn't love you."

"You don't know anything about it."

"I'm the one who loves you."

"Bert—"

"Have a potato chip?"

She shut her eyes. Tears rolled down her cheeks.

He took out his handkerchief and started to wipe it over her face. "Eat up," he told her. "You'll need your strength. Remember: you've got a big seduction ahead of you."

"Don't."

"Why not?"

She pushed her plate away and threw her crumpled napkin beside it. She shoved her chair back. He put his hand over her wrist. "Stay a little while," he said. "I've missed you."

She shook her head; she was going to get to the door if she had to drag him after her. She tottered to her feet. He took away his hand and let her go. "I'll be in touch," he said.

AS BEFORE, he rang the bell when the clock showed the precise moment they had named. This time he brought her some flowers. She asked him in and took his coat. She apologized for the state of the room, which was neater than it had been at any time since she'd started going out with Bert.

He followed her in to the tiny kitchen. She reached up to the cupboard where she kept the vases: one big, the other small with a chip at the base. She brought down the large one and started to spread the flowers out on the counter.

"I think my son is in love with you," he said.

"He's too young for that kind of thing."

"Oh, I don't know. Anyway, he can't stop talking about you."

"Well, I hope he's saying nice things."

"Sure. But that wasn't what struck me so much. It's that he's obsessive. Can't stop. Just like me."

She laughed, but the mention of Eric brought him unpleasantly into her mind. She remembered the strange dream she'd had that night when she'd stayed at her aunt's house. "Do you dream a lot?" she asked.

"Not a lot. Sometimes. I dreamt about you the night I met you."

"You did? That's amazing. I dreamt about you, too."

"What was your dream?"

"You first."

"Oh, I just dreamt it the way I wanted it. I rang the door bell, but when you answered it you were wearing one of those nightgowns you can see through. Filmy. You opened the door, you invited me in and then you took off the nightgown and we got down to business for hours and hours. It was a wonderful dream. What was yours like?"

"Part of it was mixed up with a book I'd been reading. But there was a scene in it that was more or less like yours."

"All that sex? Really?"

"Except that we weren't in the same house." And it hadn't gone on forever, without changing; but she didn't want to tell the rest of the dream.

He said, "I used to have a repeating dream when I was a child. A nightmare. That's what I think is going on with Ricky. He has these fears, but he doesn't restrict them to the hours when he's asleep. He tries to get into them consciously and change them around."

"What was your nightmare?"

"I'd dream that I was in my room, lying in my bed. The realistic detail, you see. And I'd look over at the window, where I'd suddenly notice a black shape."

"What kind of a shape?"

"That's what was so frightening. It was just like darkness. It had no . . . There wasn't really any form to it. And it was coming to get me. I used to wake up screaming."

"How old were you?"

"Seven. About then. That's when they started."

"It was a dream about death. I used to get them around that age: being chased by fire, or about to drown, or falling."

"Or flying. It's all supposed to be about sex."

"Not when you're a child."

"Don't be too sure. But children grow out of those dreams. And so did I. Then one afternoon—when I was in college—it came back. I must have been studying for exams or working too hard, or something. I got through college by working nights, taking all kinds of jobs. Anyway, I fell asleep for a while one afternoon. And when I woke up, it was nearly evening. I looked over at the window and—there it was, in my life again, my real life: the black shape, coming to get me. That was the worst dream I've ever had. It was so bad that I haven't thought about it again till now. I didn't want to remind myself. I was afraid that it might come back."

"It might not ever come back, now that you've talked about it."

"What I don't understand is that in the dream, I set myself up. I engineered something horrible for myself: I made myself believe that I wasn't having a dream. I changed the setting from my childhood bedroom to a college dorm. That was meant to convince me that the threat was real. Why?"

"I don't know. All I can think of is that you were afraid of something again and that your dream plugged you back into the old story, but it updated your surroundings to fit with your grown-up life. Has it ever come back since then?"

"No. But after the double whammy, I don't know what else it can do to me. Of course that's what I thought before, too."

She dropped one of the flowers. He bent down to get it. She leaned over at the same time. He got the flower and kissed her while she was still off balance. "Are you nervous?" he asked. "Maybe we should go to bed now and worry about dinner afterwards."

"Maybe we should finish doing the flowers."

"Maybe not," he said.

She hadn't imagined such a quick bypassing of all the stages usually considered necessary before a first night that wouldn't be the only one they'd spend together. But she had already established the fact that she was a nice girl; this was no longer the first date, she'd cleaned the apartment and changed the sheets and towels and she was hoping that the evening would end in the bedroom. That was what she was prepared for. So did it really matter if they skipped two or three hours?

Of course it didn't matter. However, since she'd been keyed up to begin with, the rearrangement of all her plans and thoughts flustered her so much that she just dropped everything and let him take over. She left the flowers scattered around the kitchen and she forgot to put the chain on the hall door.

WHILE THEY were still in bed, wondering whether they should get up and go out to dinner, or wait a while longer, the phone rang. That was another thing she'd forgotten: to unplug the bedroom extension.

She said, "Let it ring."

He reached over, picked up the receiver and waited. There was a click that they both heard, and then the dial tone.

"Wrong number?" he asked her.

"Wrong man," she said. "I've told him it's over. I kept on telling him, but he's checking on me. At least, I think so. I don't know who else would be calling. Especially like that, just to see if somebody's in."

"Burglars?"

"Not around here. We've only ever had daytime break-ins on the ground floor. Nothing at night."

He didn't seem to mind the thought that she'd only recently been attached to another man. According to his son, he'd been going out with someone else himself for the past couple of weeks. Perhaps he hadn't even broken it off yet. Or maybe Eric had been making the whole thing up.

He got up to phone the restaurant from the living room.

While they were putting their clothes on, he asked her to marry him. She said, "You don't think we should spend a little more time getting to know each other?"

"Would it help?"

"Well, otherwise—if we're living together and if we don't really understand each other's moods and what you could find irritating and everything—"

"We'd find that out as we went along. Isn't that how it works?"

"I don't know. I don't know how it works." He did: he'd been married before. She'd have liked to know whether his first marriage had been settled with such speed and boldness.

He said, "Are you telling me that you don't want me?"

"Of course I want you."

"Then you will?"

"Well, yes."

"What a great answer: Well, yes. I love it."

"When?" she said.

"If you can get off work the day after tomorrow, we'll go to the Town Hall and register. They're closed tomorrow. After that, it's a little while—I think maybe two weeks."

"But that's so fast."

"Why not?"

"Oh, everything. I mean, my family, my job, um."

"You want one of those long engagements?"

"Wouldn't it be better?"

"No. Why wait? I went through a long engagement once. All it does is make you restless and impatient. And the honeymoon's even worse. We could take a spring vacation somewhere, instead. How about that?"

"Venice," she said quickly.

"Oh? You do have it all mapped out, after all."

"I've just always wanted to go there."

"Fine. So, it's yes?"

Yes, she said: it was yes.

During dinner they hardly spoke. And afterwards he said that if she didn't mind, he'd leave early in the morning because he didn't like the idea of Ricky waking up and finding that he wasn't in the house. "In fact," he said, "if you can get off a little early tomorrow, I could pick you up and you could come home with me. We could all have tea together. Ricky keeps asking to see you again."

"Okay. Sure. That would be nice."

"And on Saturday—would you mind coming down to my ex-wife's place? She's got the right to see him on Saturdays. You might as well meet them. The vipers. They got away with a large chunk of money they weren't entitled to, and one-seventh of my son's life that they also have no right to. He won't speak to them. He takes a book. But every Saturday he has to get in the car and go. At least the two boys won't be there. Ordway was married before, too. This time should be relatively okay. They usually send somebody to pick Ricky up. But every once in a while I do the chauffeuring, just to check that things are all right there. Would you mind?"

"Not at all," she said. "That's fine." Already she was jealous. She wanted to know what his ex-wife looked like. She wanted to know everything about her, especially if it was derogatory.

In the morning, after he'd gone, the phone rang. She hesitated before answering. If Bert were at the other end, she didn't want to talk to him. But the call might be from Roy, to tell her something he'd forgotten or to change the time, or the place, for that afternoon.

She picked up the receiver and said hello.

Her Aunt Marion's voice said, "Sandra? I'm so sorry to bother you. I didn't wake you up, did I?"

"No, I was up already. Has something happened?"

"Oh, it's stupid. I'm always so careful. But yesterday morning the newsboy didn't get the paper on to the doorstep—it landed on the path. So I walked down the steps and I didn't notice that there was a little patch of damp leaves on one of them."

"Are you hurt?"

"I fractured my kneecap. It's still in one piece, but they're going to operate: they'll put pins in it, to stop it from pulling apart."

"Are you still at home?"

"I'm in the hospital. They thought it would be better to keep me here—less uncomfortable. Everyone's very pleasant. And the food is quite nice. Fortunately I'm insured for absolutely everything. But it does annoy me."

"Can I do anything for you, Aunt Marion?"

"I was just about to ask. If it's no trouble, it would be a big help. But there's no hurry. Any time before Tuesday will do."

"How about Sunday?"

"That would be perfect, dear. Let me get my list." She told Sandra the name of the ward she was in, gave her directions for driving to the hospital and read out a list of the things she'd need from home. When she had finished, Sandra remembered the phone call from the night before; maybe it hadn't been from Bert, after all. She asked, "Did you try to get hold of me last night?" Aunt Marion said no, she'd been sleeping like a log all night long because of some medicine they were giving her. "To stop the pain," she explained. "It doesn't really work. I mean, it just puts me to sleep."

She hadn't realized until she saw him that she'd been apprehensive about meeting Eric again. She'd been thinking that he'd blame her. Although his manner was subdued and well-mannered, she felt that she ought to give him some kind of apology before the afternoon was over. He didn't seem nervous himself. On the contrary, after saying hello, he asked her, politely and confidently, "Would you like to see my room?"

They started up a wide, curving staircase. Like the rest of the house, it was bigger and more important-looking than anything she was used to.

"I'm sorry about the other night," she said. "I felt badly about turning you in, but I didn't see what else I could do."

"Yeah, I know," he told her. "It's okay." He headed towards a door that gave off the landing, saying, "It's this one." He stood back for her. She walked in.

It wasn't like a child's room, nor like a place where a young boy lived. The furniture, the colors of the materials, the curtains, all looked as if they had come from the room of an adult. Even the bed was an adult's single bed with a carved headboard. Many of the objects and pieces of furniture had the appearance of expensive, well-cared-for things. They might have been antiques.

Over the small desk hung a religious painting. As her eyes went to it, he said, "That's Saint Catherine."

The picture too looked old, as did the little desk with its green leather top that had a floral pattern stamped in gold around the edges. She took a step forward.

There were three people in the painting: two women and a baby. One woman held the baby, while the other one stretched out her hand towards it. The baby, with a little help from its mother, was putting a ring on a finger of the extended hand.

"Mary and Jesus," he added. "It's called *The Mystic Marriage*. It's sort of like, ah, you know when nuns get married to God?"

"What?"

"They're given a wedding ring."

"Uh-huh. Are you all religious? All the family?"

"Nobody in the family. I saw this when my father was buying a set of chairs and I asked him to get it for me, for my birthday."

"That must have been a pretty big present."

"He said it would have been cheaper to buy me a car. He thought it was a waste of money."

"Because he didn't think it was beautiful, or because you don't go to church?"

"What I like about religion are the stories. They're pretty weird, but it's surprising how they can have an application to everyday life."

"I don't know. What I never liked about Sunday School was that they told you all that stuff that wasn't true."

"If it has an application, it's still got some truth."

"I guess I mean the thing you start out with."

"That would be a composite."

"Oh. Like how do you mean?"

"A myth or a folktale."

"Exactly. Not true events."

"But they could be."

"But they aren't. They're just made up."

"They're only made up in that they're typical. They're typical of certain wishes held by the people who tell the stories. Since we all still think the same way, those stories still typify something true."

"Like what?"

"Revenge, murder, miracles and all that sex stuff."

"Well," she said, at a loss how to go on, "I never thought of it that way before."

"It's a very interesting subject. I'm also interested in those preachers that get everybody to give them money to save their souls and then have to go into a psychiatric hospital when they're found out."

"Those people are frauds."

"They want to be demagogues."

"Yes."

"But they're using the wrong propaganda. The real power is in the secular branch."

"Absolutely," she said. "And besides, they let you keep the money afterwards."

"Right. And even if you get sent up the river, you can write a bestseller about it."

She started to laugh. He joined in. It was going to be all right, she thought. He didn't hold her betrayal against her.

He sat down in a straight-backed chair at the side. As he did so, he motioned towards the modern swivel chair at the desk. She sat down in it. She gave it a little swing, first one side, then the other. It was fun. The chair must have been another thing he'd asked for.

He said, "Are you his girlfriend now?"

"I guess I am."

"I told you so, didn't I? I said he'd be able to take over everything without any trouble."

"It doesn't mean I don't like you too. You're the one I met first."

When Eric reached the age of twenty-one, she thought, she'd be thirty-one and Roy would be forty-five. She was closer in age to the boy who would be her stepson than the man who was to become her husband. That was a strange fact. It made her imagine that the odd tale with which Eric had introduced himself to her—the story about a body-swap—could become true at some future date: that at a certain age she might say to herself that her husband was immature, whereas his son was more like a grown man.

"Is something wrong?" he asked.

"No. Why?"

"You look like you're having trouble remembering a phone number."

"I was trying to figure something out. But it won't ever happen, so I guess there isn't any point wondering about it."

"Oh, I think those are some of the most interesting thoughts of all. You know: what would happen if a meteor collided with the moon; or how would you react if you found an escaped tiger in your living room: was it that kind of thing?"

"Not so wild, but that's the general idea. Maybe everything's like that until it happens. If you're thinking about something you have no experience of."

They had tea in a smaller room off the large, high-ceilinged dining room. By the time they sat down it was dark outside. Roy accepted a cup, but didn't drink it. He sat watching her and Eric the way a man might relax to the sound of music. Sometimes he joined in the conversation, but he didn't try to guide it. Eric was the host; he told a succession of jokes and puns. She countered with her cousin's story about the hat and the Dalmatian. And after that they got on to the subject of movies.

She met Debbie, who came out of the kitchen to shake hands. Eric looked on with an expression of resignation. He didn't appear either frightened or desperate. Everything still seemed to be all right.

In the car Roy said, "You have an amazing effect on him."

"Let's hope it lasts."

"What did you think of his room?"

"It's beautiful."

"But peculiar. Like a museum. Everything antique, except for his computer over in the corner. Most of it was his mother's. He fought tooth and nail for it during the divorce."

"The swivel chair's modern."

"He didn't let you sit in it, did he?"

"Sure."

"Jesus. He won't even let me sit in it. It's his thinking chair. What did you talk about?"

"About religion. We were looking at the painting above the desk."

"The girl marrying the baby? Christ, yes. That horrible thing. It's worth a fortune now. When I bought it for him they thought it was workshop of John Doe and now it's supposed to be the guy himself. But I guess they could change their minds again. I told him he should sell it before the price drops back down. And he looked at me like I'd suggested using chemical warfare on a maternity ward."

"He loves it."

"He could love a photograph of it just as much, and invest the money he got from the original."

"A photograph wouldn't mean the same. A copy wouldn't either. From the way he looks at it you can tell that he really appreciates everything about it. I think it's like a person to him. He sits at the desk and sort of communes."

"My God, now I've got two of you," he said. "I'm outnumbered."

THE NEXT DAY, Thursday, they went to the Town Hall. On the way back he dropped her at the office, where she handed in her notice to quit, told Maureen the news and got ready to go out to lunch.

"Have lunch with me," Maureen ordered. "I'm paying."

They were outside, walking quickly in the cold air, when Bert came running up behind them. He caught hold of Sandra's arm. "We've got a date," he told her.

"No."

"Yes. I asked you Monday when you could make lunch and you said Thursday was all right."

She was about to deny it but suddenly she recalled the sight of Bert looking through his appointment book to find a free day. She'd made the date just to get rid of him.

"Want me to go on ahead?" Maureen said.

Sandra nodded. She turned back to Bert. "I'm sorry," she

said. "I forgot. I can't. Let's say goodbye, please. Don't keep going on and on like this."

"This guy—the one with the car? I asked about him and he's bad news. He did something—"

"What?"

"I don't know, but everybody says he's just no good."

How childish he was, she thought. Everybody was. Was it likely that he'd approve of the man she was planning to leave him for? But that was why divorcing couples always considered each other emotionally ill, insane, possibly genetically warped—that explained the unacceptable, which was that people changed: nothing was for long. Life itself didn't last and the changeableness was natural, like death.

"I don't want to lose you," he said. "I get this terrible feeling in bed, that I've got to have you holding me. And then you aren't there. And nothing feels right."

She started to cry. He meant more to her, now that they were breaking up, than he had for all the months that they'd been together. There had been many times when—offended and bitter—she'd wanted the power to make him feel bad, even to hurt him seriously. Now she had it and she didn't want it. She didn't want to hurt anyone like this, least of all him.

He held out his hand to her but she pushed it away. She said, "I can't. I've told you. I told you every nice way I could. We're getting married. We've already decided when. We've been to the Town Hall and everything. We've set the date."

"When?" he asked.

"In a few days."

"When?"

"Look, Bert, there's no point in this. I don't want you to get the idea that you're going to show up at the ceremony or something."

"Me?"

Of course that was what he'd be planning. She tore herself away from him, ran to the corner and crossed the street. She didn't look back and she didn't slow up, although she sensed that he wouldn't be following her. He'd be standing where she had left him, watching, while she kept on running.

Maureen didn't ask about Bert directly. She just leaned across the table and said, "Okay, shoot. The uncondensed version, please."

As Sandra talked, she started to think that everything was going to be easy. Maureen seemed to believe that the whirlwind romance was just fine—that the speed with which Sandra was being carried towards the altar was a sign of true love, and that the best news of all was that she'd be getting rid of Bert, who'd always taken her for granted and never treated her very well, especially that time when he'd had the affair with Melanie what's-her-name in accounting. Sandra agreed. She pretended to be in control of all her actions and feelings. She hadn't known about Melanie or any other girl. Maybe there had been more than one. It didn't matter now.

"Have you met his family?" Maureen asked.

"Oh, yes. Well, part of it. I'm meeting the ex-family on Saturday."

"Right. One of those. Are there any kids?"

"One. A boy. He lives with his father."

"Wow. I don't know how I'd handle something like that."

"You never know. It's only when things happen: then you

find out. That was the trouble with Bert. Nothing was ever going to happen. I always thought he was nice, but it wouldn't have worked. He just wasn't the right one. Now that I've made the decision—God, I don't know how I stood it for so long. I should have gotten out of the job, too. This place: don't you feel it? It's hard to find anybody in that building who isn't one level lower than a computer."

"I love it. I'd go crazy living with people who only wanted to talk about the weather and the kids. I like things fizzy."

"So do I. I never felt that way about the office, though."

"I feel that way about all offices. That's why you're getting married and I'm not. Some girls grow up dreaming about making hubby his breakfast and bouncing the baby in its basinette; I always had this craving for filing cabinets and typewriters."

"You're kidding."

"The great thing about offices is: there's no mess, no clutter, no smell of boiled cabbage, no cockroaches and—best of all—the people there don't yell at each other all day long. Wall-to-wall carpets, warm in the winter, cool in the summer, somebody else does the cleaning, everyone's friendly and polite, they like the way you do things, they give you money: there's a lot to be said for it."

"But not all marriages—"

"You can never count on things for long. And it's always easier to leave a job than to walk out on a marriage."

"But if you love each other—"

"Sure. That's what they say: it makes all the difference. That's the part I left out."

• • •

SHE LET everyone else in the office know that she'd be leaving. Most of them didn't need to be told: Maureen had been spreading the word. She telephoned her sister and then her parents, who sounded stunned, as if she'd done something alarming. Their reaction upset her. Didn't they think she was ever going to get married? The girls in the office had the right idea: they approved. They seemed to feel that getting married was in the same category as winning a million dollars in the sweepstakes. Even Maureen, who didn't have much to say for married life, thought that it was the right thing for Sandra.

Her parents asked her how long she'd known him. They didn't like her answer. Her sister, too, kept saying, "Are you sure?" and then added, "What happened to that nice boy you were sort of living with for a while? The Ivy League type. Bert."

"That was a long time ago," she said.

EARLY ON Saturday morning she drove to Roy's house. His car was outside. Eric was sitting in the front seat, behind the wheel. She parked in back of him, got out and walked over. She leaned towards the window. "Are you driving?" she asked.

"Not yet. He's on the phone. He told me to stay outside."

"I'll just let him know I'm here," she said.

She found Roy standing in the hall. He was holding the telephone receiver to his ear and saying, "Yes, yes."

She whispered, "Do you want me to wait in the car?" He nodded and made a kiss at her. She went back outdoors.

They had a pretty, sunny day for the trip. It even seemed to be a bit warmer. Everything they'd missed in the spring was coming to them now. She got into the passenger seat next to Eric. He was wearing a shirt and sweater: on the back seat lay a folded jacket with a hood. It struck her that every time she'd seen him, he'd been wearing different clothes. That was the way rich people lived, even the children. But for a child to dress that way meant that someone else must choose his clothing. Did Roy do that, dragging his son along on shopping expeditions?

"That's in case we go for a walk," he said. "We probably will. My father likes to get out of the house as fast as he can. The beach is okay."

"Do you two go shopping for your clothes together?"

"Why?"

"I was always taken shopping by my mother. She'd grab a lot of things off of the racks and push me into a dressing room with them. I guess she had a very good eye. Usually they all looked fine, so then she'd just ask me which one I liked best and she'd buy that one for me. But my sister couldn't stand going with her. They used to have fights. She didn't like any of the clothes my mother chose. She wanted to wear silver jackets in the daytime and that kind of thing."

"That's what I'm going to do as soon as I'm sixteen. He says I have to wait till then. Sometimes he makes me come along with him. About once a year, mainly for shoes. You have to try them on. Everything else I pick out of catalogues. Once you know your size, it's easy. Then I show him the picture and most of the time he says yes. I know the kind of thing he's going to want me to get."

"That's the first step."

"Is your sister grown up now?"

"Oh, yes. She's a couple of years older than I am."

"What does she wear?"

"Pants and a turtleneck, mostly. And black eye make-up around her eyes; no lipstick, long hair. And she won't wear shoes in the house: she doesn't like them. But that's as far as it goes."

"How do you mean?"

"She's not really a rebel. She doesn't want to be anti-social and break things up. She just couldn't stand to have somebody else making decisions about what she was going to wear and how she was going to look: anything about her appearance. She has to be the one to decide."

"Well, that's the way I think, too. Don't you?"

"Not really. I don't always mind when other people decide for me. Sometimes it saves a lot of trouble. There are loads of things I don't care about one way or the other."

"I always care."

She laughed. "I know you do," she said. "Listen. Do I call you Eric now, or should I call you Ricky?"

"They're both no good, specially Eric. They called me that because when I was born I had red hair, so they thought: Wow, Eric the Red. And they named me after that."

"But it's a good name."

"It's a twerp name. Your name's okay. I bet you weren't named for a joke."

"It's all right now, but my real name is longer. It's Alexandra."

"Alexandra? Jees, are you lucky. That's great."

"It's too long."

"It sounds like the name of a princess."

"It probably was. My mother was reading some novel

around that time. She told me she got it out of a book. We all have to put up with things like that."

"But you got a good one."

"So did you. If you ever go to Scandinavia, you'll be surrounded by Eriks. Over there it's like the name Richard. And meantime, you can call yourself Rick. Like Rick's Bar, you know."

"What's that?"

"It's from a movie. There's a nightclub owner in it named Rick. He's the hero. He wears a white tuxedo and he's a cool customer."

"Oh?"

She looked up as Roy came out of the front door and down the path. "Who gets to sit in front?" she asked. "Or can we all squeeze in together?"

"Not in this car. It's only got seatbelts for two in the front seat. You stay there." He got out and climbed in to the back. Roy took his place behind the wheel.

THE HOUSE they pulled up at was a new, low-slung beach cottage on the outskirts of town. Many glass windows and doors allowed for the maximum incursion of light. The beach wasn't in sight, but you could hear it.

Sandra made an immediate move to ingratiate herself with the ex-wife, Ginette. "What a light room," she said, looking around as if pleased. She already felt relieved by Ginette's appearance: bleached hair, tight skin and an expression of casual toughness.

"I like things clean, with plenty of light," Ginette said, looking at Roy. "No dark corners."

Sandra said, "My grandparents lived in a house that was so

dark, it was hard for more than one person to read the news-papers in the dining room. I used to think it was gloomy but I started to appreciate it later on, when I was working with computers and my eyes began to hurt. I guess all they really needed was better electricity."

The husband, Ordway, was introduced: an agreeable, sloppy middle-aged man who wore thick glasses. He seemed perfectly happy to have guests. He greeted his wife's ex-husband without concern and appeared to be undismayed by Eric's atrocious manners.

Eric wouldn't look at, or speak to, either the wife or husband. He took his book over to a chair by one of the windows.

"Still not on speaking terms?" Ginette called after him. "That's a long time to sulk, kiddo. A couple more years of that and you'll be batting even with your father." She turned to Roy, saying, "Want a drink?"

"No, thanks. I'm driving."

"Not even one little drink?"

"Tonic water?" Ordway suggested. "Ginger ale? Orange juice?"

"Tonic water," Roy decided.

"My," Ginette said. "A reformed character. And you?" she asked Sandra.

Sandra asked for a light gin and tonic. Ordway mixed the drinks and did the serving. He took a ginger ale to Eric, who—without raising his eyes from the page—extended a hand to have the glass inserted between his fingers; the operation went so smoothly that it looked like an established ritual.

How would I act, Sandra thought, *if he ever treated me that way? I wouldn't be able to stand it. And his own mother: what did she do to make him hate her so much? She left. Maybe that's all it was. She wanted out, so now he's showing her that he can do it back, even when they're in the same room.*

"Such marvelous manners," Ginette said.

Roy slapped his drink down on the table and stood up. He said, "I think I'll stretch my legs." He started to move towards the doors that led out on to the terrace.

Ginette turned to Sandra. "Have you had any experience with children?" she asked.

"Babies?"

"No, a little older. Eric, for instance. How well do you know Eric?"

Sandra paused for a second, not wanting to say anything that would hurt the boy. "About as well as I know his father," she said. "How well do you know him?"

Another moment passed before she realized that she'd said something brilliant that didn't necessarily have to be taken as an insult. Eric looked up from his book for the first time since he'd sat down. He laughed. And Roy was grinning.

Ginette didn't try to hide her displeasure. She said, "Better than you, I think. But you'll find out."

Roy said, "Coming with me, Ricky?"

Eric looked back down at his book.

"Well? Are you?"

"Rick," Sandra prompted under her breath.

"Coming, Rick?"

Eric shut the book and put it aside. "Sure," he said. He walked to the doors.

Sandra watched father and son step out on to the terrace and begin to walk away. There was no polite way of getting up and following them. She was stuck.

"I know what it looks like," Ginette said. "It isn't the way you think. I did my best, God knows. I knocked myself out, trying to help. But that boy is a demon." She set her drink down on the table in front of her. "Just like his father," she added.

She's still in love with him, Sandra thought.

Ordway looked over at her glass. "Another drink?" he asked. Sandra shook her head. He reached for Ginette's glass. She put her hand over the top of it. "I'll see about lunch," he said.

He walked around to the side of the bookcase, opened a door there and left the room.

Sandra hung on to her glass tightly.

Ginette said, "So. How long have you two known each other?"

"Not long at all."

"Yeah. Well, you're taking on a bundle, I can tell you."

Sandra looked towards the windows. She could see Eric, far away. He seemed to be throwing something at a point that was beyond her range of vision. As she watched him, Roy came into sight. Looking at both of them, she thought that there was nothing to worry about. She felt fine about them. What bothered her was simply the idea of marriage at such short notice: it was like stepping off a cliff and hoping that something would be out there in front of you.

"Let me tell you a story," Ginette said. "I've got a cousin whose sister-in-law studied to be a forest ranger. They do a lot of botany, looking at things under microscopes and so on. And then they go through the woods and make reports. She had an assignment to record growth patterns in a certain section of forest. It meant measuring the treetrunks; they did that regularly all the time to check the rate of growth and line it up with what they knew about rainfall and sunshine and temperature averages. And the way you do it, if you're making a routine survey, is to put your arms around the trunk of the tree. That gives you an approximate figure. Well, she was doing that for a while, taking notes, moving from tree to tree and she didn't notice, but—somebody else was there too, because all of a sudden she put her arms around the next treetrunk: and from the other side of the tree someone grabbed her wrists and started to pull. They pulled her right up against the trunk and pulled and pulled until it felt like her arms were going to come out of their sockets. And then, just as she thought she was going to pass out with the pain, whoever it was let go and ran away. Luckily. She was so exhausted that she wouldn't have been able to defend herself in any way. She just dropped down on the ground and shook all over. She didn't see who it was. She didn't think of trying to look. Her arms hurt her for weeks."

"And she didn't have any idea who it could have been—a stranger, or somebody who might have followed her?"

"No idea, except that it was a man, of course. A woman wouldn't have had the strength. It's a funny story: she was just minding her own business, going along as usual, and—wham."

"It's a horrible story."

"That's what can happen, even when you're not expecting it. That's what men are like. Not all of them. Ordway's a sweetie. But most of them. In fact, I really used to wonder about Roy and his first wife. Don't you?"

"I thought you were his first wife."

"No, honey. I was his second wife."

"Who—"

"The one that was Eric's mother. The millionairess who was twice Roy's age. And she died in such mysterious circumstances."

"Oh?"

"Oh, did she ever. Ask him about it. If he won't tell you, you can find out by looking up the records. It was in all the papers."

From the distance Roy and Eric ran towards the terrace. The wind blew their clothes and their hair.

Ordway put his head around the bookcase corner. "Soon?" he said.

"I can see them coming," Ginette told him.

During the meal Eric kept his head down and ate. Sandra led the conversation. She hadn't meant to, but the first bite she took drew her to comment; the words burst from her like a blunder. "My God," she said, "this is amazing. I've never tasted anything like it. What wonderful food." She looked at Ginette, who said, "Not me. Ordway's in charge of the kitchen."

Sandra turned to him. His smile showed such pleasure at her appreciation that it was as if all at once they were alone together, two friends at a table of strangers. She said, "This is much more delicious than just good cooking. Have you studied somewhere?"

"You could call it private tuition, I guess. My grandfather was a famous chef. I never realized how much he was teaching us when we were children. We were all supposed to grow up to be something on Wall Street. But when I think back, he did have us organized like a team of apprentices and he'd vary the menu all the time. We were building up a repertoire without knowing it."

"Was he French?"

"Polish."

"You never told me that," Ginette said.

Ordway shrugged. There was a slight pause. Sandra was afraid that it might turn into an unbreakable silence. She asked Ginette to tell her something about the house.

Ginette began to talk, at first lazily, then with gusto and at last rhapsodically, about the dream she'd always had of living in that part of the world. She'd been on a school visit to the other side of the bay and she'd never forgotten it. She'd always wanted to have a summer cottage there. And later on, she'd begun to look for a place, but nothing matched the dream she'd had of the perfect house. Then, one day, she was browsing through the magazines in her dentist's waiting room and she saw an article on modern American architects. There was a picture in it of a house that she liked. Everything started from there. She knew at that moment that she'd have to begin from scratch: buy the land and hire that architect to design the house she wanted.

The story of the building, with its setbacks, triumphs and surprises, lasted till after dessert. They were back in the living room with coffee before anyone thought of changing the subject.

Roy had remained silent throughout the catalogue of dramatic events. *He's remembering the divorce settlement,* Sandra thought, *and he's telling himself, "They did all this building and buying on my money."*

Roy said, "We'll be getting home early, if you don't mind. There's a lot to do."

"Could we take a little walk on the beach first?" Sandra asked.

"Sure," Ginette said. "We'll all go."

Sandra tied a scarf over her head and put on the gloves she'd brought. The wind had picked up, the sun was going behind clouds. Eric ran ahead of everyone. Ordway took Ginette's hand. He led her straight out from the house, towards the water. Roy hung back.

Sandra said, "They've gone off to compare notes about us. And now we're going to talk about them."

"What's she been saying to you? When we came in before lunch, you looked like you'd been hit by a truck. What was it?"

"Why didn't you tell me that he isn't her son?"

"Oh. I didn't?"

"You know you didn't. Why?"

"I guess I thought you'd figure it out. You're somebody I don't have to give explanations to."

"But if she's got part-custody, of course I assumed that she was his mother. I could have said something terrible."

"But you didn't. You've played everything fine."

"But I could have." She didn't understand why he'd let her go on thinking something wrong. Had it been a test? Or had it been like a joke—the kind of thing Eric had worked out when he rang the doorbell at her aunt's house?

"What else did she say?" he asked.

"She said I should ask you about your first wife."

"Uh-huh."

I'm asking, she thought. Why had he done this to her? He

must have known how important it would be to her. Perhaps he hadn't been able to tell her himself; he'd arranged things so that she'd have to ask. Or wasn't it that complicated?

"Okay," he said. "I'll tell you later."

He'd have to tell her soon. She didn't like the thought that some day her suspicions would drive her to the public library, where she'd sit at a table and turn over page after page of old newspapers, seeing his face looking out at her. Maybe there were photographs that showed him trying to cover his eyes with his arm, or putting his head down as two policemen hustled him through the crowds. *It doesn't matter,* she told herself. *It happened, but now it's over.*

She breathed in and turned her face to the sea. "I really like the beach," she said.

"Me, too. So does Ricky. If it weren't for those two, he'd be having a good time here."

"Maybe he'll look back on it later and think it wasn't so bad."

"Not a chance. One thing I can tell you right now: as soon as we're married, we can drop old Ginette from our list of social engagements. The reason she got what she got was that her hot-shot lawyer made a case for a child needing a steady, maternal influence in his life."

"That's me, huh?"

"You got it. Oh, and there's some bad news, I'm afraid. Ricky's dug in his heels about the wedding. He wants to be best man, you know. So apparently—I don't know whether it's the clothes or what, but he's insisting on a church wedding."

"You're joking."

"No."

"My God. Which church? I haven't been inside a church for years."

"I don't think I've ever been in one, at least not for the reasons you're supposed to. My father was a devout atheist. Whenever anyone brought up the subject of religion, he'd say, 'It's a bunch of crap.' It was his favorite expression. I can still hear him saying it."

"And your mother?"

"Oh, she did what he wanted. You know."

She remembered the painting of Saint Catherine in Eric's room. She asked, "Does this mean we've got to go through some kind of embracing-the-faith thing?"

"Hell, no. We just get some laid-back preacher to let us use his church for the party."

"From what I picked up when we were looking at the painting in his room, he might like a lot of authentic stuff: a Mass in Latin and—"

"There are limits. He can have the church ceremony, but that's as far as it goes. If you don't mind, that is. Does your family go to church?"

"Not any more. My mother's family were Congregationalists, I think."

"Okay. Are you game?"

"I guess so. I'd rather not."

"We can pretend it's like being in a play. I think we're going to have to go to rehearsals for it."

"Are they going to ask us if we believe in God?"

"Probably. You just say, 'You betcha.' "

"That's what I'm saying when they ask me if I take you for my lawfully wedded husband."

"That's what I like to hear. We'll sail right through it."

During the drive back Eric was talkative. It was as if he had to make up for his long silence. He wanted to play word games, to ask riddles, to talk about the lemurs of Madagascar; he'd read a long article about them in the *National Geographic* and he'd heard somewhere else that people were supposed to be descended from lemurs, not monkeys.

Sandra was interested. That was a good sign, she thought. If he didn't irritate her after a day of nervous anticipation, that was an indication of future compatibility.

It was dark long before they reached the house. She drove her own car home. Two hours later Roy arrived to take her out for the evening. They went to a seafood restaurant where there was a dancefloor and a band that played the kind of music people used to dance to: foxtrots, waltzes, tangos and the Charleston. They didn't speak about the afternoon until they were sitting in the car, outside her apartment block.

He said, "Ricky's completely changed. He's like a different boy. You know, it wouldn't matter if he didn't, but I can't tell you what a relief it is to me that he likes you so much. He's taken to you like . . . it's like magic."

"You've said something like that before."

"Can't say it too often."

"It's beginning to make me a little nervous. I already don't want it to change. It's still such a short time since we met."

"That's not important. It's getting better and better. Here, let me show you something: this is how the state foresters measure trees. What's wrong?"

"That was the other thing Ginette told me while you and Rick were out walking. The story about the girl who was going through the woods and had her wrists grabbed."

"I think it's a story that has some special significance for her. She didn't tell it to me till about a year after we were married. But you got it the first day. And that fuddy-duddy, Ordway—you practically galvanized him. Both of them, spouting away on their pet subjects. I think they were even having a good time."

"So was I, looking back on it. At the time I was too panicked to have fun."

"You should have been in public relations. People open up to you. Don't they? Just like flowers."

"Not usually. And not the other way around, either. It's because I'm in love."

"You weren't in love when Ricky made friends with you."

"But I'd just seen a very romantic movie the night before. And I was reading one of those love stories where they're all wearing costumes."

"I see. That explains it. The girl who absorbed romance. It should be a headline."

"But I meant what I said this afternoon. I liked Ordway a lot. I think it's a good thing he got out of his old job. He's an artist. And I certainly admire what Ginette did with that house."

"That god-awful futuristic thing?"

"It's good."

"Post-fifties Americana—lots of style and no character. Wouldn't you rather have one of those ramshackle wooden houses with a shingle roof?"

"Oh, I would for myself. But that doesn't mean that there shouldn't be other types of houses around. I wouldn't want to live in the Empire State Building either, but I think it's great. And it isn't just the house. It's the fact that she had a dream about doing something and she carried it out."

"That's Ginette, all right. A schemer."

"I admire people who are well-organized and good at planning. Rick's like that. Whatever else is going on inside him, he's able to make a clear plan and then act on it."

"Sometimes his plans are a little crazy, that's all."

"I'm no good at planning. Everything in my life has just happened to me."

"Then I guess it's not a bad thing that somebody else is going to be in charge of the wedding arrangements."

"That's true enough. I don't even know how it all works: bridesmaids and invitations and—God, everything. Even the dress. My sister had a registry office wedding. So did my cousins. Nobody in my generation ... Well, I guess my mother would know."

"If you don't mind, Ricky's sort of set his heart on running the show. The whole thing."

"Are you kidding? I thought you sort of hired people."

"He's going to do all that. He's even got a fixed idea about the kind of wedding dress you should have. He showed me a picture."

"Oh, boy."

"Do you care? It would mean so much to him."

"Okay, sure. If he wants to make all the arrangements, that's fine. I'd kind of like to see that picture first."

"I think I've got it with me. Wait a minute." He turned on the ceiling light. He looked through his wallet. The picture wasn't there. He reached into his breast pocket and pulled out a paper. "There," he said. "That's it."

She unfolded the paper. She'd expected to be handed a glossy photograph out of a fashion magazine. What she saw was a pencil sketch of the head-dress and veil from the portrait of Saint Catherine.

She handed the paper back to him. "It's from the painting in his room," she said. "Don't you recognize it?"

He frowned at the picture. "I think you're right. I hadn't noticed. It isn't bad, though, is it?"

"Not at all. It's beautiful."

"Good. You'll just be kind of medieval. He made an appointment for you to have the first fitting on Monday morning. And he wants a list of guests. And what about bridesmaids?"

"There's my friend, Maureen, from the office. And my niece and nephew; they're still tiny, but they could hold up the train, or whatever they do—carry some flowers around."

"Don't forget to invite that old aunt of yours. She's our fairy godmother."

She thought that before they kissed goodnight, he'd tell her what he'd promised earlier in the day. But they went up to her apartment and went to bed. He was getting ready to go back to his house, still with no intention of saying anything, when she realized that unless she made a move, he'd never do anything about it.

"Please," she said, "tell me now. You've got to, sometime. I don't want other people hinting at me. Tell me yourself. Tell me about your first wife."

"I just don't want to think about it."

"Good. Neither do I. All you have to do is tell me, and then we won't either of us have to think about it again."

"Okay. Right. Well, most of my immediate family succeeded in killing themselves while I was young: in car crashes, getting sick, looking for fights and getting beaten up, suicide—that was only one. I was put in the care of . . . it's not important."

"That's all right. I want to hear everything."

"I guess it was an act of kindness. Maybe that was why I resented it so much. The community thought it would be a nice idea for one of its decent citizens to give me shelter for a while. So the local optician took me in. But by that time it was too late: I had a grudge against everybody. I didn't like the way they'd always treated my family. I was very busy biting the hands that fed me. So he took me in and I took him in. I seduced his wife. That would have been all right up to a point. Mutual advantages. But when I won the scholarship and was on my way to the station, she staged a terrific farewell scene. She was a lady of great, suppressed dramatic talents. Threw herself down on the ground and confessed all in terms that would have embarrassed Casanova. The doctor got out his pistol. He managed to shoot a hole in a little glass-shaded lamp they had and she was all over him, screaming, "Oh, don't hurt him, don't hurt him." And I ran for it. The only reason this is of any interest is that later on, when I needed as many character references as I could scrape up, the good doctor made it his mission in life to try to send me up the river without a paddle. He got into a plane and came all that way voluntarily just to tell the jury what a conniving, cold-hearted rascal I was. And it didn't do me any good."

"She must have suffered a lot after you left."

"Don't you believe it. She had a good time with me. And after I'd served my purpose, she had the supreme pleasure of throwing it in his face. You could see why she wanted to, too. He wasn't the kind to forget an injury, or an oversight, or a misunderstanding, or a mistake, or a badly ironed collar. Anyway, I had the scholarship. I was working nights and looking for weekend jobs. I bought a second-hand pick-up truck and I used to move furniture for people, fix their washing machines, clear the leaves out of their gutters, put the storm windows on, mow the grass—anything. That's how I met Harriet. Something had gone wrong with her gardener's back. He needed some extra help with lifting things. In other words, he'd talked her into hiring another man to do his work, while he stood there and gave his mouth a lot of exercise. But we got along all right. I worked there for a long time. It was one of my best places. And I got to know her. She was famous. She owned art collections and gave charity balls and all that. She had millions. You wouldn't have thought it; she looked like an ordinary woman, nobody special. She was forty-three when I met her. I was almost twenty."

"What did she look like?"

"Medium height and build, short brown hair, going gray. She liked golf and tennis. When she was younger, she used to ride. And she had a pilot's license. Her family was unbelievably moral and upright for people who'd made millions. She'd been brought up in some old-style ideal of Christian service that made her feel uplifted about life. She was a good sport. Good company, even though she was teetotal—that was another of their things: no liquor, tobacco, coffee.

"One day there was a fire in the kitchen. We got it out, but when I took a look at the place, I could see it was the wiring. The whole house needed to be rehauled."

"Go on."

"I'm late. I should be getting back."

"Not till you tell me. Please."

"Right. She'd never had a lover. It's hard to believe that people still live like that, but some do. I asked her to marry me and she said yes. We were fine together; she was fun. I liked her. She wanted to get married fast, so we did. When I met the rest of them, I understood why. You've never seen such a gallery of stuffed shirts. Of course they hated me. And they thought I was a fortune-hunter, which wasn't entirely untrue."

"But you didn't marry her for her money."

"Not entirely. But partly, yes. Of course. Why not? It wasn't as if I was planning to walk out on her. I thought we'd be on friendly terms forever. And things went very well. The family had to admit that I made her happy. And then, four years later, when nobody was expecting such a thing, she got pregnant. That was when I began to feel regret—remorse—for the way I'd behaved, because the doctors were all horrified. They didn't think she stood a chance. They said that the baby was sure to be mongoloid or deformed, or that something would go wrong because of her age. According to them, she shouldn't have considered pregnancy after the age of thirty-five. A couple of them suggested an abortion.

"She just swept all the advice aside and said that she felt well and happy, and she was looking forward to bringing up a child. I was scared. I didn't think she'd make it. She was forty-seven. Even after it was too late for anyone to have done anything about it, they kept telling me how dangerous it was for her. But she was laughing. And when Ricky was born, we were both laughing. When she made me hold him in my arms, I was just overwhelmed; all the years I'd stopped feeling any kind of sentiment: and suddenly it caught up with me. He was smaller than I'd imagined he'd be. And he had a lot of wild red hair. That was when I started to love her.

"She turned out to be one of those natural mothers, who take it all in their stride and enjoy it. But of course I was seeing other women, off and on. I was also working hard, going up in the world, making a name for myself, making money. Once I'd made enough, people stopped thinking I'd married her for mercenary reasons. And then: the night of the accident. She'd invited about a dozen people for dinner, maybe a few more. About fifteen. For the past year she'd been giving fantastic dinners where she'd have the table decorated like a kind of bower, or a temple, or a bandstand. I don't know what it was supposed to add to the evening; I'd come home from work and find myself sitting down to a meal where I had to keep batting rosebuds out of my soup or wondering if a white dove might fall off its perch and land in the salad. Most of these evenings were given over to fundraising for charities, so I guess maybe there was an element of showmanship to them. Harriet used to hire all sorts of designers and interior decorators to help her.

"On this particular evening, she'd had a glass pipeline laid down the table and overhead. It curled up, all over the place. The pipes were filled with water. Colored tropical fish swam through them and they were illuminated by a series of lights that were made to look pretty rather than functional. There was a fountain in the middle of everything and a lot more of the lights. The overall effect was intended to be one of an under-sea treasure-cave.

"Well, I got home early but I went straight upstairs. I looked in on Ricky, took a shower, and when I came downstairs, the guests were already arriving. So, the first I saw of this Disneyland table arrangement was when I went in to dinner with everybody else. And the first thing I said was that it looked very nice, but was it safe? 'Oh, yes,' she said.

"I started to check it—all you needed was one loose connection and a little spilled water, and the whole house could be alive. I was still fussing around at my end of the table when I heard her say, 'Just this little wire,' and then she screamed. Half the other people there started screaming too. For a minute it was hard to tell what was going on."

"She was electrocuted?"

"That's right. It's a wonder we weren't all incinerated. Apparently the only bit of metal casing that could be dangerous was right in front of Harriet's place at the table, where she was bound to notice it. The people who'd been responsible for setting up the equipment said that everything had been completely safe but that I had degrees in all sorts of things and, since I'd been in the house for hours, I could have tampered with it. Well, the police thought that that sounded reasonable. I was under arrest and hiring lawyers. There were two hundred reporters camped outside the doorstep. They wouldn't even leave Ricky alone. And then, the trial: dear old Dr. Danforth getting his chance to dump all over me; I really wished I'd taken the opportunity of laughing in his face before I made my getaway from under his roof. They all thought I'd done it but they couldn't prove anything, so they had to acquit me. For months afterwards I got letters, telling me that I'd gotten away with murder but that everyone knew I'd done it just the same. Do you believe me?"

There was something in the story, some part of it, that wasn't true. She'd been waiting so hard to find out how the wife had died, that she couldn't remember where the moment had come, when she'd heard it in his voice, and had thought: *He's lying.*

But did it matter? She didn't really believe that he'd done anything, merely that he might have wanted to. The important question, she thought, was not what terrible things people did, but whether you loved them or not. Since she did love him, he might have done anything at all and it wouldn't change things for her because her love was like faith: it wouldn't allow her to accept any other truth. Only the loss of that certainty could make her believe that he'd killed someone. What he wanted to know was whether she loved him.

"Yes," she said. "Of course."

HER CAR whizzed along the beltway with the outbound traffic. Every once in a while she looked at the speedometer. Bert had always let himself be pulled in to a faster pace, without realizing what he was doing, especially if he was thinking about something else. He'd switch his mind off and follow the crowd; and she'd sit there, not saying anything, but wanting to.

She thought about a church wedding. Maybe the idea wouldn't have thrown her so much if she'd been given a little preparation. Everything was going fast; that was the way she wanted it, but it seemed dangerous. Years ago, when she'd been trying to choose between two apartments, she'd felt the same mixture of exhilaration and dread. It was as if the more certain she became, the more there was bound to be something wrong with the place. Why was it like that? It didn't make sense. It ought to be the other way around. All doubt should vanish, once you knew.

She reached Aunt Marion's house early, let herself in and packed up a tote bag with the things on her list. Before setting off again, she went into the living room. She sat down in the chair where, just a few days ago, she'd been reading: when the doorbell had rung and there outside had stood a small boy in a suit and tie. It was unbelievable. But after it had happened, it was a fact. And after that it was normal, although possibly still crazy. She should relax. Lots of people did the wrong thing and it turned out all right anyway.

She checked the house, locked up, hid the key, carried the bag to the car and drove out to the hospital.

Aunt Marion looked different; she didn't like being in a hospital, yet she approved wholeheartedly of the nurses and doctors who, she said, "couldn't have been kinder." Already she knew all about them: their hopes, their dreams, their families. She seemed inordinately pleased and touched that Sandra had taken the time to come to see her.

"I'd have come before," Sandra explained, "but you said that there wasn't any hurry, and I've been so busy with all kinds of things. Aunt Marion, I've got some news. I'm getting married."

"My dear, how exciting," she said. "Was that what you had to think over while you looked after the house for me? After you crossed the other one off your list?"

"In a way it was connected with that. I had to decide what I felt about the man I was turning down. It's so strange—just as I made up my mind, my future husband appeared. He's the father of that little boy who was lost—the one who ate up everything in your kitchen."

"Wait now, just a minute. Don't say anything more for the moment. I'm a bit scatterbrained nowadays." She rang the bell by her bed. "Let me settle down. I'm supposed to have a cup of tea at about this time. Will you join me?"

Two nurses looked into the room. Aunt Marion ordered tea from them as if she were in a restaurant. They chatted and joked with her. She was evidently a favorite patient, despite her old-fashioned ways. She introduced Sandra. The nurses were named Carroll and Reba. Carroll had a high, twittering voice and giggled a lot. Reba was tall, ironic, and she gave the impression that she wouldn't stand for any nonsense. "You're slipping down again," she said. Aunt Marion leaned forward to let her plump up the pillows.

"Sugar and cream?" Carroll asked.

"Sugar and milk," Reba told her. "She already said. And a slice of lemon. Okay. Anything else you need?"

Aunt Marion said no, and thanked them. The nurses left. Sandra still felt like an outsider, as she had from the moment when the two had entered the room.

"I can't understand it," Aunt Marion said.

"What's that?"

"You've known this man for no more than a week?"

"That's right. But that's enough to tell."

"And this is the man whose first wife died in that hideous way? Everyone thinks he murdered her, you know."

"What everyone thinks isn't always true and it doesn't matter anyway."

"It doesn't matter?"

"It isn't important what people think. They don't know anything about it except what the yellow press puts out to boost their circulation."

"Oh, no. It was in the real papers. The big ones."

"I love him," Sandra said.

"I don't doubt that. But in any marriage there's also the question of suitability, particularly after the initial infatuation wears off."

"It isn't going to wear off. It's going to become deeper and stronger and more wonderful."

"With a lot of work on your part. Men never try to make a marriage go. It's unfair to expect them to. They have other interests. They like comfort, but they also like novelty. Almost as fickle as boys: suddenly they're off and away to something new. Even though Hudson was always good as gold, I was glad that I had the foresight to keep an old admirer of mine up my sleeve. It didn't mean anything, naturally, but if I'd ever needed something to tease Hudson with, it was there."

"Aunt Marion, those are such sexist ideas."

"Yes, dear. I expect that's just why they work."

Sandra tried to laugh. She said, "You sound as if you disapprove of marriage."

"Not at all. On the contrary. I simply think it's a mistake to hope that it's going to be something it couldn't possibly be. It isn't heaven; it's merely a way of life."

"Surely it's heaven to spend your life with someone you love."

"If you're not suited, that life together can destroy the love."

"But how do you find out if you're suited? You get married."

"Sandra, you mustn't think I'm against you when I say these things. I'm very worried for you."

"There's no need to be."

"You've known him barely a week."

"Yes. I hope you'll be able to come to the wedding."

"That depends on when it is."

"As soon as possible."

"The child—what's his name?"

"Rick. Eric."

"Do you think he's a jealous boy?"

"No. He's accepted the marriage. In fact, he seems to be delighted by it."

"I meant—when you have children; how do you think he'd take that?"

He might cut them up to see what was inside.

"I don't know. I don't really know how I'd take it myself. I've put off thinking about a lot of things. I'm just going to have to worry about that later."

"I have an idea that they may keep me in here for a time after the operation. After that, I could be in a wheelchair or maybe on crutches, with a cast. All very awkward. But you'd understand if I didn't come, wouldn't you? Everything can be such an effort when you're not feeling well, even if you're looking forward to it."

"Of course. But I'd miss you."

"Well. What would you like for a wedding present?"

"I can't think. I've got everything I want."

"Yes, that's one good thing: you won't have money troubles. She was fabulously rich. They say that's what he killed her for."

"Oh, Aunt Marion, how can you? He's a brilliant man. He's made more money on his own than she ever had."

"Starting from what she left, and using that to back his ideas."

"He could have asked any big corporation to put up funds for him."

"Perhaps."

"Definitely. Anyway, if he's supposed to have killed his first wife for money, I shouldn't be in any danger. He's the one who's rich. I don't have much of anything except my car, and that's all beat up."

"Yes, that's a blessing. But you might quarrel about something. About other women, for instance."

"Really? Why would we do that?"

"Because that was part of the story. He even invited the other woman to the dinner where it happened. I suppose he felt obliged to marry her afterwards. But she wasn't the only one."

"He didn't murder her either, did he?"

"It's possible that she held something that might be used against him."

"Oh, for heaven's sake. Well, in that case, it's also possible, isn't it, that she was the one who killed the first wife?"

"No. She didn't have the technical skill."

"She could know enough to take the insulation off a wire."

"Ah. So you have read up about it, after all. Why did you do that, if you were completely sure?"

"I didn't. I asked him about it and he told me: it was an accident."

"I see."

"If you wanted to give me a present, what I'd really like is something you've made yourself. When you've got time. Something to wear, or something for the house."

"Oh. All right. That's easy."

"I was thinking last week that I might give you something, but I forgot to ask you about it. Aunt Marion, have you ever wanted a cat? A kitten?"

"Oh, not after Catarina. You never knew her, did you? I'm afraid I'm a one-cat woman. And at my age, I really don't want the worry. No pets whatsoever, please. Not even a guppy."

There were footsteps in the hall. The door opened and Reba announced, "Teatime, ladies." Carroll followed her with a tray that she set up on the bed. Sandra pulled her chair forward.

Aunt Marion said, "Thank you, girls. That looks just fine." She told Sandra, "Reba's getting married, too."

Reba said, "That's right."

"Are you nervous?" Sandra asked.

"The way I look at it, if you never take a risk, you might as well be dead. Got to take a chance sometime."

"That's what I think, too. And if it doesn't turn out to be what you thought, you can deal with that later."

"Right."

"Nothing's ever exactly what you expect, anyway."

"You're telling me." Reba gave the pillows one last push and turned to go out with Carroll. "Chip off the old block, your niece, ain't she?" she said. "You'll be okay, honey."

"Good luck," Sandra told her.

"Uh-huh. Likewise."

Aunt Marion said, "It's not the kind of tea I like, but it's not too bad."

"It's nice that there's one person at least who agrees with me."

"That's entirely different. Any man who tried to kick up a fuss with Reba would find himself in the emergency ward before he knew what hit him. She's no shrinking violet."

"Am I?"

"Oh darling, of course. Stars in your eyes, head in a whirl after one week. It's heartbreaking."

"It's what I want."

"I had gathered that. And I do appreciate the invitation. Sandra dear, I wish you many, many years of happiness."

"Thank you, Aunt Marion."

"But if it doesn't make you happy, please feel free to come and cry on my shoulder at any time. I'll try hard not to say, 'I told you so,' even though it's always such a temptation."

"I might be the one to say it to you."

"Now that's a much better idea. That would please me enormously. You're the only younger person in the family who seems to be even partly recognizable as a member of the human race. I mean—well, you know what I mean. Is your sister still doing that thing to her eyes?"

"The kohl?"

"Last time I saw her, I thought she'd walked into a door."

"I like it. I think it brings out the color in her eyes. And it makes them look bigger."

"And she doesn't wear any lipstick at all. She's too pale."

"She hates lipstick. Aunt Marion, she has her own style."

"Well, we all have that."

"And some of us have enough for two," Sandra said, putting her cup back on the tray.

Aunt Marion laughed lightly. She held out her arms for Sandra to kiss her goodbye.

•   •   •

AS HER PANIC GREW, the formal pattern of events helped her to look at them as if they were normal. Things were proceeding as they were supposed to: she invited her bridesmaids, spent hours talking over the telephone, shopped, put her apartment up for sale. The burden of emotion might have been heavier if she'd had to deal with her own family interfering on the spot, but her parents didn't think that they'd be able to fly in until the very last minute and her sister gave the impression that the wedding couldn't have come at a worse time. "How much would it matter to you if I didn't show?" she asked.

"It wouldn't matter at all to me. Mom and Dad are the ones who'd hit the roof."

"Well, that's nothing new. I just wouldn't want you to feel bad."

Sandra said again that she wouldn't mind.

If her sister did turn up, her mother would find an opportunity of criticizing whatever she'd chosen to wear. There might be open hostilities. At a time when every detail had to be right, it would undoubtedly be better not to have both of them together.

She tried on her wedding dress, in which—despite the unusual design—she felt extremely bridal. As she stood in the center of the floor with her arms up, the dressmaker and her assistants worked deftly over the sleeves, back and neck. She turned around, put her arms down, moved to the left and to the right. They knelt on the floor. While two remained busy near her, the third would go farther back in order to judge the effect. It was like watching people trying to hang a painting; this time, she was the picture. All three of them were amazed by the quality of the materials they'd been given to work with. You couldn't find lace like that any more, they told her—not anywhere. And the veil, they said, was beyond belief.

When the last pins were out, the last stitches in, one of the girls said, "Oh, you look just like a swan," and another one added, "You can't have even one extra spoonful of cottage cheese between now and the big day. Those seams stay where they are."

On the morning of the first fitting Roy asked her if she'd like a new car. At first she said no, but when she saw how much he wanted to give her one, she remembered what trouble she'd always had with the old rattletrap she'd been driving for years. She'd bought it second hand and she'd never owned another car. She said yes. The excitement and pleasure of this new toy drove many other things from her mind. She forgot, for instance, about the ring; that is, about the engagement ring. The wedding rings were already being sized.

"Would you like something brand new?" he asked her. "Or antique? From an estate jewelry collection—that kind of thing? Or would you like to see a ring that's been in the family?"

He'd already described his parents as the sort of people who'd never had much of anything. If there were rings in the family, they'd have belonged to his first wife, Harriet, and now—presumably—to Eric. She said, "If we had enough time, we could try everything. But if you have something in mind already, maybe you could show it to me now. It might save us a trip in town."

"That's what I thought. That's why I had it made the right

size when we were choosing the other rings." From his jacket pocket he took a box, opened it and handed it to her.

She took the ring out of its box. The elaborately carved gold was set with three diamonds: two matching stones that flanked a center one of slightly larger dimensions. Wherever the light hit them, they played it back.

"Do you like it?" he asked.

"I've never seen anything so beautiful."

"They're not as bright as modern diamonds because they're the old cut—not so many facets. But the stones are tops."

"They look plenty sparkly to me. Would you put it on for me?"

She handed the ring to him. He put it on her finger. They both looked at it. It was obviously the right ring. He kissed her.

She asked, "Was it Harriet's? I don't mind. I'd just like to know."

"It belonged to one of her aunts. It's not very old: about 1910. But Ricky thought it was the prettiest one and he made a big point of how practical it would be, because it wasn't too big, so you could wear it in the daytime and not think that somebody was going to mug you for it."

"I love it," she said.

ALTHOUGH—as Roy said and as Eric had told him—the ring wasn't too large or too showy to wear every day, she was conscious of it all the time. She kept looking at it. When the stones were hit by direct sunlight, they blazed. Under artificial light they sizzled and glittered as if generating brilliance and color, unaided, from within. She was fascinated by them. Her mother's engagement ring had never caught the light like that, nor had her grandmother's.

All the girls at the office loved the ring, too. At the party they gave for her, one of the secretaries yelled above the babble of voices, "Hey, Maureen says you're marrying a billionaire. Does he have any brothers?"

"No brothers," she said. "And if he had any, they wouldn't be anywhere special. He's a self-made man." She smiled, as if she'd been paid a compliment.

"Gee," the girl said.

She'd been waiting for someone to mention the money. Bert hadn't said anything, but Bert would know that the money wouldn't be important to her. Now, for the first time, she wondered how true that really was. It would certainly make everything easier. She would have her own space, lots of it; and physical comfort and all the freedoms people didn't have when they were forced to limit their spending. That easiness would become a way of living. "It's just luck," she said. "I'm glad about it, but I'd want to marry him no matter what."

"Yeah," the girl said, "that's better than money. But it's never lasted with me. Six weeks and it's like you can't believe you were so dumb."

"It's different when it's for keeps," she said, adding graciously, "You'll see, when it happens to you."

SHE WENT to the church with Roy and Eric. The officiating clergyman for their service was to be a Reverend Eustace: a large, plump man whose air of primness was offset by good humor and a tidy-minded efficiency that broke down periodically as he forgot where he'd put things. The most troublesome article he owned was his pair of reading glasses. He'd never needed spectacles until a few months ago, he explained to Roy. Now he had them and he couldn't find them.

"This never used to happen to me," he said. "I've always thought of increasing age as a time of aches and pains, but in my case it seems to be this ridiculous forgetfulness. It started with the glasses and it's spreading to other things. I keep finding myself over in a part of the room and I can't remember why I got up to go there, or what I was looking for. The glasses used to be a real problem until I discovered those ordinary magnifying glasses they sell in drugstores: they're almost as good. So now I have four pairs. But there are days when I can't put my hand on any of them."

Eric was sent off to check the places where the flower arrangements were to be set up. He also wanted to ask some questions about baptism and funeral services. A dark-suited man named Bates took him in tow.

Reverend Eustace ushered Sandra and Roy into his study. He sat them down and gave them a short speech that left enough margin for them to express approval about the goodness of man without having to lay claim to any specific brand of religion.

It came as a relief to Sandra that she wasn't going to have to lie. Despite the Reverend's appearance, he was on home ground now and, once the door had been closed, it was—she felt—a little like being called to the principal's office. She didn't have either the effrontery of Roy, who was prepared to say anything in order to get what he wanted, or the honesty of someone like her sister, who had once told an interviewer that she wanted the job because she needed the money.

If asked, she was going to express regrets about her lapse from churchgoing. And if she tried, she could convince herself that that was true. She would have liked to believe.

The chair she sat in faced a windowframe that had been given a shape she recognized as religious. The books in the bookshelves, the cross on the wall, even the Reverend Eustace, put her in mind of the way she'd felt about religion as a child. It had seemed to her, a long time ago, that there was a special sweetness—a rightness—in adherence to a certain way of life and a lovely perfection in its precepts, which you could aspire to but never fully live up to.

Reverend Eustace offered them each a sherry and poured one for himself. "I'm sure everything will go exactly as planned," he said, "although if it doesn't, there's nothing to worry about. If there's a hitch, just remain calm and wait. I've seen people catch their clothes on the door, get their heels stuck or slip on the carpet and fall over. The children can wander off. If there's a baby in the audience, you can bet it's going to cry. Someone drops the ring. And so forth. All perfectly normal. The important thing is that the bond should be made, the words should be spoken and understood and that the union should be consecrated by a man of the cloth in God's presence."

"Of course," Roy said. He knocked back his sherry without changing expression. Sandra knew that it wouldn't be dry enough for him. She and the Reverend had a taste for sweet things.

"But some quite extraordinary things can happen," Reverend Eustace murmured.

"Like people getting up to complain," Sandra said, "when you ask them if anyone objects: 'Speak now or forever hold your peace'?" Suddenly she thought about Bert. She imagined him shouting out for everyone to hear: *This woman once spent three days in bed with me and we weren't reading the Bible to each other, either.* Memory, combined with the alcohol, rushed the blood up into her face.

"It's interesting that you should mention just that place in the ceremony," Reverend Eustace said.

"Well, it's the one everyone waits for. You think it's going to be like the end of *Perry Mason,* where somebody stands up in the courtroom and says, 'I did it.' "

"As a matter of fact, there was a story going around last year about a case where the proceedings were interrupted at that very point. It happened in a church down south. Everything was going according to the schedule until the minister said those words. There was a silence—you know, you have to leave a little pause—and then he was about to go on, when the bride herself spoke up. She said, 'I have something to say.' She turned around to face the congregation and she said, 'I'd like to thank all the people who've worked so hard to make this moment possible: my mother, who organized the food; my aunt, who arranged the flowers; my sisters, who helped with the catering; and my bridesmaids.' She stopped and the preacher was about to continue, when she took a breath and kept going. She said, 'I'd like to thank all my friends and relatives who've come here today, some of them from far away, to wish me luck.' She stopped again. And once again the minister was about to resume, but she turned around a third time, and said, 'But what shall I say of my matron of honor, who went through school with me, and who spent the summers with us all through college, who's been just like one of the family all these years: and who slept with my bridegroom last night?' And then she picked up her skirts and marched right out of the church."

Roy said, "I bet that was a bad moment for the matron of honor's husband."

"And the mother," Sandra said. "All that food, waiting for the guests. I hope she stood up and said, 'Never mind, everybody. The party's still on.' "

"Ah," the Reverend said. "That's what I really like about that story. Everyone has a different point of view about it. Some wonder what happened to the bride afterwards, others want to know if the groom tried to go after her."

"And you?" Sandra asked.

"When I heard the story last summer, my first thought was for the clergyman, of course. Such a dreadful thing to happen in your own church. In God's house."

"If He made us," Sandra said, "He must know how badly we can behave."

"You can know a thing and yet not want to have it aired in public."

"That's right. We're the ones who mind, not God."

"We mind because of Him."

Roy said, "My fiancée forgot to tell me she was an expert on theology."

The Reverend Eustace smiled smugly. He was the expert.

Sandra laughed. She put up her hands in a gesture of capitulation. She still thought that she was right.

Mr. Bates was summoned. Eric walked into the room after him. Everyone was supposed to memorize the moves and the timing, and to remember where each person was to stand. Reverend Eustace gave Sandra a piece of paper on which her cues were written.

They went through the questions and answers. Eric said, "I didn't bring the ring. I didn't think we'd need it today."

"That's all right," Reverend Eustace told him. "Just make sure that you know when we're going to ask for it."

"I know that already."

Sandra gave Eric a wink. He didn't like being told things in the tone the Reverend had used to him. He'd decided that the man was a dimwit.

"And now," Reverend Eustace continued, "George isn't here today, but I think that Mr. Bates can let us have a few notes on the organ. If the bride would wait outside?"

Sandra walked to the door. Eric fell in beside her but the Reverend called after him, "You're needed back here, young man."

Eric slouched back towards the others. Roy put out an arm and pulled him close.

Sandra sat down in a pew at the back of the church, where they'd left their coats. The others followed later, gathering together up near the altar. She was glad of the chance to observe without taking part. She especially liked watching Roy and Eric together. They looked happy, she thought.

She was blasted out of her reverie by a roar from the organ. As more musical notes followed, Eric walked away from the others. He came down the aisle to where she sat. She couldn't hear him above the noise. She cupped her hand behind her ear. He gestured towards the door. They picked up their coats from over the back of the pew, opened the door and went out.

They walked down the path and to the sidewalk.

"I don't think that guy is very well organized," Eric said. "Do you? He spends a lot of time telling you things you don't need to know."

"He told us a terrific story while you were looking around the place with Mr. Bates."

"Typical. He waited till I was out of the room."

"First of all, he wanted to talk to us about how serious it was to get married and what it meant. Um, the spiritual side of it."

"Oh. Okay."

"The story came up because it was about a wedding that went wrong."

"That's great. He thought it was going to make you feel good to hear that?"

"I think so. Because it happened to somebody else."

"What was the story?"

She told him, changing the wording at the end, so that the bride accused the matron of honor of "fooling around" with her bridegroom. Eric was impressed. He said, "Do you think it's true? That really happened?"

"I think so. Something pretty close to that."

"There's something I want to tell you. You know, when I rang your doorbell?"

"Yes."

"It happened like I said, that day. But I started doing it the year before, when he was going out all the time with all those women. See, I knew that he'd get married again and I

232

thought it would be the same as last time: he'd get a divorce and I'd be stuck with the ex-wife and her husband. I saw you out walking that day. You didn't notice me. You were looking down. You were thinking about something else."

Bert.

"You took your hand out of your pocket to push your hair back, like this. So I saw you didn't have a ring on. I thought you looked nice. My father . . . He never went out with anybody nice. I thought if I got to know you—well, then maybe I could ask you over. And we could all have lunch together on Sunday. Or something like that. That's all. I thought I'd better tell you, in case people said I was always going around to strange houses and acting weird. I mean, there's no point in doing it any more. I'm not a crackpot."

"I know that," she said.

"And it's okay, isn't it?"

"It's perfect," she said. "It's almost what you could call providential."

"I knew it would be okay."

"Yes," she said, smiling. "And if it isn't, it's a big house, so we can all go sulk in our own rooms."

He thought that was so funny that he had to do a little dance as he laughed.

The Reverend came up behind them, his forward movement seeming to be powered by the swell of his important belly under the clerical garb. "A time for rejoicing, eh?" he said.

"We were wondering," Eric told him, "what would happen if you forgot your lines."

"My goodness, I hope there won't be any need to worry about that. We might have to do it all over again."

• • •

THERE WAS no time left. She'd spend an hour thinking, *I'm getting through everything so well, with such businesslike capability, that I'm going to have plenty of time left over.* At the end of that hour she'd wonder if she was ever going to make it.

Her family arrived. The first thing her mother said to her sister was, "Couldn't you find another hat?" Her sister turned right around and left the hotel room, slamming the door as she went. Her father said, "Oh, dear." He said it frequently in the following days. As the wedding ceremony approached, his nervousness took the form of a furious and abnormal need to shake hands: everyone he met was pumped by the arm not simply at the moment of introduction but whenever he felt friendly, which was often, as he was also, unusually, drinking a lot. He remained charming while he became slow, sleepy and slightly hard to understand. "He looks like a mounted fish," her mother said.

Her sister helped to dress her on the wedding day. "You look fantastic," she said.

"I feel really out of it."

"Did you drink too much last night?"

"I didn't drink anything. I didn't dare. I keep worrying that I'm going to fall over. God, I wish we'd held out for the registry office."

"You're actually going to renounce the devil and all his pomps?"

"I think that one's in the baptism."

"I'd go for the pomps every time, sweetie."

"But you didn't."

"That's only because it wasn't among the choices being offered."

No, Sandra thought, *you wouldn't anyway.* As she watched her sister holding up the veil, carefully brushing the edges straight, she felt very proud of her stubborn, independent spirit, her stoicism and the way she chose to live her life by principles that she wouldn't even bother to discuss; she had married a man her parents disapproved of, lived in obvious, bohemian squalor and seemed happy with him and their children.

Sandra asked, "Did you have any doubts before your wedding?"

"None. But I had all that massive family outrage to keep me steady. It's harder for you. They think he's wonderful."

That was the way it looked, certainly; everyone except Aunt Marion. Aunt Marion's knee hadn't healed quite so quickly as the doctors had hoped. She wouldn't be at the church after all. Sandra had known that somehow, at the last minute, her aunt wouldn't be able to attend: she didn't want to. After a certain age you had the right to keep away from what you didn't want to do and to save your strength for things that were fun.

"How about the kid?" her sister said.

"What about him?"

"You think that's going to be okay?"

"It's fine," she said. "In fact, it's all great. If only I can get through today."

"I'm glad you're doing it all the right way. It makes up for how disappointed they are in me."

"It's only Mother who feels that way. And the reason she

does is that she expected so much more of you. She never thought I was worth bothering about. It's true. And the reason she gets so mad is that she envies you. She'd have liked to live like you, but she never dared. She's always been frustrated. You showed her that it would have been possible, if only she'd had the guts."

"You're kidding."

"That's the way it always seemed to me. You're the one she admires. Anyway, she's getting a little better."

"I hadn't noticed. Did you hear what she said about the hat?"

"I hope you're going to wear it."

"I'm not sure."

"There's nothing wrong with it except that it's ahead of its time."

"That's enough."

"I like it," she said.

The preparations, the nerves, the waiting and worrying were beginning to remind Sandra of the time leading up to a long plane flight. She kept running to the bathroom and at the same time feeling thirsty. She was drinking one glass of water after another.

When at last she stood outside the church, with her veil down and her hand on her father's arm, she was so dizzy with anticipation that she was close to fainting. Her knees felt as if they weren't going to work. Her happiness became almost indistinguishable from terror. As she thought of Roy, who would be standing by the altar with Eric, she couldn't remember what he looked like. A wave of sickness passed over her. She was marrying a man she didn't know; this was like the weddings in other parts of the world, where the couple were committed and married to each other before they were fully acquainted.

She was even a stranger to the ground she stood on. She'd been inside the building—a place for ceremony and public spectacle—only twice before. She was wearing a dress that seemed less like clothing than like a theatrical costume or a kind of location in which she was hiding, disguised from anyone who might be looking for her.

A silence fell. Then the organ started up again. Heads turned around to look. Her father patted her hand. "Easy does it," he said. She squeezed his arm. They began the long, slow walk down the aisle.

On both sides people leaned forward to look. She was grateful for the veil; although it might not hide her face completely, at least it formed a space between her and the rest of the world. Her cheeks felt tight and burning; they might almost be on fire. Her father sauntered along as if he were out for a ramble in the country. She was filled with affection for him. She regretted the fact that she hadn't gone home more often after moving away to join the office. And now she'd be married and her time wouldn't be her own.

As she passed by, she saw everyone without being able to understand what she was looking at. The only people she seemed to recognize were her mother and sister, who were sitting with their arms around each other. Both of them were crying and her sister was wearing the hat.

They reached the others. She was looking at Roy. Her father handed her over to him. All at once she was glad of everything: the strangeness of the dress, the presence of the crowd behind her, the fact that her friends and family were there to see the moment when her life joined with other lives to begin a new family. And, above all, she was happy that she was being married in a church. Religion was forever: everything else was only temporary.

Reverend Eustace began to speak. All the stages of the ceremony went as they had rehearsed it. When she was supposed to respond, she was pleased at how firm and audible her voice sounded.

The time came for the business with the ring. Her head turned. Was Eric going to drop it? Had he lost it? No. He stepped forward smartly, like a little soldier on parade, presented the ring and retreated. The blessing came next. And another handover. Roy had the ring: he took her hand. She knew that her hands would be slightly hot and swollen, but she had already mentioned that that might happen. If she just relaxed, there was no reason why the ring shouldn't fit. She looked down until it had slid over the first joint of her finger, then her eye was caught by Eric. He had moved from where he was supposed to be. He was craning his neck to see everything. On his face was an emotion she found—from behind the veil—hard to decipher, although it seemed familiar. His eyes were lowered, his posture was one of someone who waits, not patiently nor with excited expectancy, but with mesmerized satisfaction. A little smile had begun to move across his lips, changing his expression by imperceptibly accelerating degrees from the ordinary to the extraordinary, so that as she felt the ring pushed fully on, she was aware of him standing now nearly in front of her, his concentration directed wholly at her and an almost sightless look on his face: rapt, transcendent, sublime.

ABOUT THE AUTHOR

RACHEL INGALLS was brought up and educated in Massachu-setts. She has been living in London since 1965.